PHANTOMS

PHANTOMS

N. K. CARLSON   MARIE MCGRATH

ALAINE GREYSON   JINNY ALEXANDER

LO POTTER   ANDREW PARKER   GERRI R. GRAY

ISBN: paperback 978-1-7353926-5-3
Ebook 978-1-7353926-8-4

Any references to historical events, real people or real places
are used factiously. Names, characters, and places are products
of the author's imagination.

Cover Design by Diana TC, triumphcovers.com
Edited by Ashley Olivier and Brian Paone
Book Designed by Jean Lowd

First Printing Edition 2020

Published by Creative James Media
Pasadena, MD 21122

To Halloween and horror lovers everywhere

Father Gilden and the Haunting at Lord Beckonly's Estate

N. K. Carlson

T he cart bounced and jolted its passengers as it bumped along the cobblestone street. The priest held the reins loosely as the donkey pulling them was quite adept at navigating the terrain. The priest's hair was graying, and his black robe was weathered from many years of loving use. Beside the priest sat a boy of thirteen, with dark hair and eyes to match, dressed in nothing clerical. In fact, the only thing about him that betrayed his identity as an acolyte was the beaded necklace he wore, from which hung a small silver star.

The cobblestone street soon vanished, and a dirt track took its place. The donkey settled in between two ruts that carts and carriages had formed in the dirt since the last rain, and the bumping of the cart lessened significantly, much to the pleasure of its riders.

"Why are we going to Lord Beckonly's house?" the boy, whose name was Sam, asked the priest. Sam was an orphan boy raised in an orphanage until recently being selected to join the Divine Order as an acolyte.

"Lord Beckonly has summoned us," the priest told the

boy, studying the ruts in the road in front of them as well as the slightly deeper ruts coming from the other direction. "He is having issues with the demonic."

He said it so matter-of-factly that the boy hardly registered what had been said. A half a minute later, it dawned on him.

"Did you say demonic?"

"Oh yes," said the priest. "You can't expect there to be angels and no demons, can you? By the Gods, can you imagine?" He chuckled to himself at his little joke. Sam did not see what was so funny.

"When you say he is having issues with the demonic, what does that mean?" Sam asked, concerned. So far, his duties as acolyte had involved lighting candles, burning incense, and singing, and he was feeling rather nervous about this new development.

"Well, it's really quite simple," the priest replied as if explaining an easy sum. "Things are moving when they should not be moving, funny noises, feelings of dread, that sort of thing."

"Good gods," Sam exclaimed.

"Yes, and thank the gods they are good," the priest said, nodding gravely. "The gods will protect us as long as we are in danger."

"So, what are we supposed to do about it?" Sam asked. He had no idea how one removed a demon, let alone several if that was what it came down to.

"What do demons hate most in the entire world?" the priest asked, beginning the rhythm of one of their learning sessions when Sam learned all about the gods.

"Uh …" Sam searched for the right answer.

"Faith," the priest said, providing the clueless Sam with the answer. "Demons cannot stand even an ounce of faith, so that is what we are bringing." He patted a wooden box that was placed next to him on the seat of the cart. "Faith in abundance."

Sam looked at him like he was out of his mind. He was so flabbergasted that he had no question to ask and so fell silent.

The donkey continued at its slow, leisurely pace up the path out of town onto a wide country lane. The cart maintained its position inside the ruts quite neatly. Trees towered over them and shaded them from the sun. Presently, they came to a fork in the road and took the path to the right. After a brief mixture and mess, the cartwheels again settled neatly into ruts on the path.

A few minutes later, a large ornate gate stood before them, open. The guard house was empty. The priest urged the donkey onward, and they went up the drive traveling in the well-worn grooves. Sam saw a large manor house, built of stone and vaguely resembling a castle but looking shabby, as if it needed a good dusting.

They disembarked from the cart, and the priest took up the wooden box in his arms. The donkey stayed put with no urging. The large wooden front door looked imposing and immovable. The priest took the knocker in hand and knocked thrice.

After a short pause, they heard footsteps on the other side, and then the latch of the door turned, and the door swung outward. A young woman greeted them.

"Father, please, come in," she said, bowing slightly to the priest. "Right this way. His Lordship and Her Ladyship are expecting you in the library." The priest stepped forward across the threshold, and Sam followed suit.

The stone passageway was lit by torches along the wall. The light from the torches illuminated faded tapestries that once must have been elegant and vibrant. The servant girl turned to the right into a room, and when Sam stepped in behind the priest, he found it was a large room with shelves along all four walls. The shelves were roughly half full, but even half full, it was clear that the room was home to hundreds of scrolls and leatherbound books. Sam turned slowly in awe, looking at all of the books and thirsting after the knowledge held within.

"Father Gilden, so nice of you to join us," a voice said from the middle of the room. Sam turned again to see a man seated on a carved wooden chair that resembled a throne. The man was nearly bald, with a severe looking face. His clothes were fine, yet clearly far from new. Beside him stood a tall blonde woman in a red evening dress, elegant but slightly faded by time.

"Lord Beckonly, thank you for inviting us," Father Gilden replied, giving a slight bow to their host. "And Lady Beckonly, always a pleasure." He inclined his head to her. "This is my acolyte, Sam," he said, gesturing to Sam with his right arm.

Sam stepped forward and bowed to the lord and lady.

"You have this one well trained in courtesy, Father," Lord Beckonly remarked.

"Not trained, no," Father Gilden said, looking at Sam with a twinkle in his eye. "No, Sam here is as true and noble as they come."

Father Gilden stepped forward to sit on a wooden chair across from Lord and Lady Beckonly and gestured to Sam to do the same, which Sam obliged.

"So, tell me," Father Gilden began, "Why have you summoned us here?"

"Well, Father, there have been some strange occurrences in our house as of late," Lord Beckonly said. "Odd noises, things falling off of shelves when no one is around, objects being moved, chills in the air."

"And you suspect a supernatural cause to these phenomena?" Father Gilden asked.

"I am a skeptical man, Father," Lord Beckonly replied with pride in his voice. "I am not easily won over by, well, by your sort of thing."

"And by my sort of thing you mean belief in the gods, angels, demons, miracles, those sorts of thing?" Father Gilden replied with a question, but it was phrased like a statement.

"Well, er, yes," the lord said, appearing uncomfortable. Sam couldn't help but notice that Lady Beckonly looked rather more uncomfortable than her husband. Father Gilden seemed to also pick up on this too and addressed his next question to her.

"And what say you, Valerie?"

He said much more with what was left unsaid. Sam had come across Valerie's name in the clerical records at the temple. Her family had been among the most devout in the area for centuries. Father Gilden's sort of thing, as Lord Beckonly put it, seemed to be exactly her sort of thing too. Or it had been. She had stopped coming to the temple when she married the Lord Beckonly some years back.

"Well," Lady Beckonly said, "I have noticed some *unusual* things." Her eyes widened as she looked to Father Gilden. Sam wondered if there was more going on behind her eyes. She seemed to be pleading.

"What unusual things have you seen, my lady?" Father Gilden asked, leaning forward toward her.

"The same things my husband saw," she replied. "I think we have a ghost or a poltergeist."

"Is that so?" Father Gilden said, leaning back and tapping his fingers together. "What makes you think it to be a ghost or a poltergeist? Please, my lady, be as descriptive as possible."

Lady Beckonly seemed to reach deep within herself for extra resolve, and then she shuddered, as if something were fighting within her.

"I feel them, Father," she said, looking at Father Gilden, her face now as white as a sheet. "When I am in a room alone, I feel the eyes on me. The hairs on the back of my neck stand up as if someone breathed a cold breath on me. But when I turn around, there is no one there."

Father Gilden sat and studied the pair of them. Sam kept glancing back and forth from the father to the lord and lady, waiting for someone to speak again.

"I think that is enough information to be going on with for now," Father Gilden said.

"So you can help us?" Lady Beckonly pressed.

"Indeed," he replied with a nod.

"What will you do?" Lord Beckonly asked.

The father hesitated. "Well, that depends upon your hospitality. I think it quite appropriate for Sam and me to stay here for the night."

"Stay here? Overnight?" Lord Beckonly stared at him, aghast.

"Certainly," Father Gilden allowed. "Based on the testimony of yourself and your wife, it seems clear to me that something supernatural is occurring in this house. I would like to get to the bottom of it."

"I thought you would light a few candles, say a few prayers, and it would be taken care of," Lord Beckonly said flatly.

"Well, I certainly do plan on lighting candles and saying prayers," the father said patiently. "But I would like to be more thorough than that. But of course, the matter rests upon your hospitality."

Lord Beckonly looked at his wife with exasperation. She narrowed her eyes at him and shook her head quickly. Their silent argument lasted a few seconds before Lord Beckonly gave up.

"Fine," he grumbled, "you may stay."

"Excellent," Father Gilden said, as if he had failed to notice the disagreement that had just passed between husband and wife. "With your leave, we will begin. Please leave us here in the library. We will, of course, walk around the house, but we shall stay out of your way as best we can."

"Thank you, Father," Lord Beckonly said, and the lord and lady left the room. When they were properly gone, Sam turned to Father Gilden.

"What are we supposed to do about this?" he asked, completely bewildered.

"Oh, there are cures and antidotes for these sorts of things prescribed in the sacred texts," Father Gilden explained. He knelt to the floor and opened the top of the wooden box he had brought with them. Inside, Sam saw a collection of scrolls, candles, oils, and incense. The father took one such scroll and rolled it out. He silently read, then rolled it back up and placed it carefully in the box.

"The gods prescribe prayer, incense, and candlelight," he said simply.

"So, what do we do?" Sam asked, still puzzled.

"We will walk the house and grounds and agitate any spirits that may be here."

"Agitate? Won't that make them mad?" Fear seeped into his voice as he spoke.

"Oh yes," Father Gilden said, with no such fear in his voice. He spoke as one speaking of weeding the garden or visiting the market. "I have never known a spirit to be happy with being exorcised."

"Is it … is it quite safe?" Sam stammered. He was liking this less and less.

"Yes," the father said as he placed a candle on a golden candlestick holder. "And also no."

Sam said nothing.

"We are safe because the gods have vowed to keep their servants safe," Father Gilden explained. "And not quite as safe as we would like because the servants of darkness wield many terrible weapons. Now, let us walk around the house."

He handed Sam a candlestick and a short chain, on the end of which was a hollow metal ball from which fragrant smoke was pouring. The father took up his own incense thurible and candle and led the way out of the library, into the hall, and out the front door. It was chilly and gloomy outside now, and dusk was a few hours away.

"As we walk, wave your thurible to and fro and waft the incense around the house. Hold your candle steady. The incense is nectar for the gods and poison for any dark spirit."

They began to walk slowly around the perimeter of the house, wafting fragrance to and fro. Sam focused closely on his task and watched carefully to see that he was matching Father Gilden's technique. They finished one lap of the house, and the smell of incense grew stronger as they entered the remnants of their previous lap. This time, Sam paid less attention to the act itself and more attention to their surroundings. The house was surrounded by forests but had about a hundred yards of clear land until the trees began. They turned along the side of the house, and Sam noticed a dirt track leading through the woods. Around the back of the house, Father Gilden suddenly stopped.

"Do you feel that?" he asked.

Sam furrowed his brows. "Feel what?"

"The heaviness," Father Gilden said simply. "You'll know it when you feel it."

Sam was confused but said nothing. They continued walking and wafting. Suddenly, their candles flickered and went out, though no breeze blew. Father Gilden handed Sam his thurible and quickly lit both of their candles again. They continued on, but Sam felt that it was much harder to walk now than it had been earlier.

"I feel it now," Sam said softly. "The heaviness."

"Yes," Father Gilden remarked. "We are opposed."

"Are we safe?"

"That remains to be seen," Father Gilden said, and a note of worry finally crept into his voice.

They went on slowly. It felt to Sam as if his shoes were caked with mud, making each step harder and harder, but when he looked down, his shoes were clean. After what felt like a half hour, they completed their second lap of the house.

"One more to go," Father Gilden said. "One for each of the gods."

The fragrance of their previous two trips around the house still hung in the air, but the heaviness only grew stronger. By the time they reached the first turn, it was noticeably darker. As they rounded the corner, Sam thought he saw movement in the trees. But when he looked closer, he saw nothing.

And then the feeling that they were being watched began to creep up the back of his neck. His skin prickled with goosebumps, and his pulse quickened. He looked around for the source of the watching but saw nothing.

"We are being watched," Father Gilden said.

"By whom?" Sam asked.

The father had no answer.

By the time they reached the back of the house, it was

nearly completely dark. Their candles were the only source of light in the gathering gloom. In the last light of day, Sam thought he saw two cloaked figures in the trees, but the darkness swallowed them up, and he was not sure if he had actually seen them or if he had imagined them. His heart hammered so loudly he thought for sure Father Gilden could hear it.

"Be brave, Sam," the father said in a reassuring tone.

The house loomed larger than ever beside them, casting shadows in the gloom that danced the dance of dead trees in the wind. After several minutes, Sam realized that neither of them had taken a step forward in several minutes. There they stood, rooted to the darkness. Upon registering this fact, Sam turned to Father Gilden, whose face was a pale beacon in the night.

"Come on," Sam said, pulling at the sleeve of the father.

"What's that?" the father asked, as if coming to himself out of a trance. "Oh, it's you Sam. Yes, I remember now."

Father Gilden falling under the spell of the dark grounds caused fear to rise within Sam greater than any previous fear. His heartbeat pounded in his ears. The sound of rushing wind filled his head, though he felt no such wind. He grabbed Father Gilden's hand and with a great effort tore his feet from their rooted spot. The father stumbled forward, nearly tripping on the grass, but soon the pair was in an all-out sprint, hand in hand. Sam felt if he let go, both of them would be lost. To where, he did not want to think.

They rounded the corner and came to the side of the house. Their momentum took them on a wide arc around the house, so much so that they had hardly straightened out when it was time to begin making the final turn toward the front of the house. There was their cart and their donkey, who was braying in terror, a sound that managed to find its way into Sam's ears.

The sight and sound of the distressed animal had a calming effect on Father Gilden. He hurried over to the terrified beast and soothed it with gentle words and a soft touch. The animal slowly calmed.

"And now," Father Gilden said when the donkey was nice and soothed, "for the house."

Sam and the father walked to the front door and opened it. The hinges creaked loudly, an unearthly wail that rattled the windows. The sound felt like a dagger to Sam's heart. The dark hall stretched before them as an open mouth ready to devour them.

"Come, Sam," the father said.

He led the way down the hall, walking confidently. Sam mimicked his steps so closely that he was in danger of walking into the father. They walked through to the library, which was dark and empty. No sooner than when they entered the room did the door slam shut behind them with a crash. Sam nearly jumped to the ceiling and began backing into the room. A sharp pain hit his back, and he whirled to find he had simply walked into a table. The father calmly walked to the door and tried the latch. It was locked. And then the door on the other side of the library slowly creaked open, though no one was there to open it.

"By the gods!" Sam cried out.

"By the gods, indeed," Father Gilden said. He opened his box, which was just where they had left it. He lit several candles and instructed Sam to set them around the room for light. Then he began to burn incense. When the smell of incense was strong, the other door slammed shut with a crash, causing Sam to jump yet again.

"They are agitated," Father Gilden said with a note of satisfaction in his voice. "There is yet hope for our errand."

"This is what you want?" Sam asked, with panic in his voice. "These spirits are angry!"

"We must be doing something right, then," Father Gilden retorted. "Now I must warn you that the spirits will do everything in their power to drive us from this place. No matter what happens, from here on out, we must remain in the house. We must not let this place be a stronghold for them. If we are unsuccessful, they will dig in deeper and be even harder to drive away in the future. As long as you are with me, you should be fine."

Sam nodded in response.

"Let us keep burning incense, then I shall attempt to speak to our foes."

"You're going to try and talk to them?" Sam asked, absolutely incredulous.

"It would be rude to not speak to them," Father Gilden said as if he were discussing a trip to the market. "I find that speaking to someone is the most effective way to find out where you stand."

The father sat down in a chair and waited. Sam sat down opposite but remained poised on the edge of his seat, ready to bolt. As the incense in the air grew stronger, the father began to absentmindedly hum a hymn.

Just then all the candles blew out, and they were plunged into darkness. Sam gripped the arms of his chair so tightly that his hands soon began to hurt.

"Father Gilden?" he asked hesitantly after a few seconds.

"I am still here, Sam, no need to fear. I will strike a match momentarily."

The seconds between the conclusion of the statement and the actual lighting of the match stretched on for weeks to Sam, but soon the fire erupted, and he could see Father Gilden's face appear out of the darkness.

"Now, Sam, I will speak to them." He paused, cleared his throat, then spoke loudly and clearly. "My name is Father Gilden, priest of the gods and the Divine Order. How many of you are there in this dwelling?"

Sam waited for some reply, hoping against hope that no one would speak. Then there was a loud thud as a book seemed to jump from the shelf and hit the floor. Then another followed it, and a third. Then it was silent. Sam felt as if ice water was flowing through his veins, and his heart pumped furiously.

"Three spirits," Father Gilden said to Sam. "Not ideal as there are two of us, but not insurmountable either." Then in a loud voice again, he bellowed, "Spirits three, I command you in the names of the gods to leave this house and never return."

A scream ripped through the air. It seemed to be coming from the hall through which they had entered the room. Father Gilden stood and walked purposefully to the door, which swung open at his approach. He paused but looked out into the hall cautiously. He held a candle in front of himself, shining its light forward. Then another scream ripped through the house, echoing off the walls.

"Help!"

The voice was that of Lady Beckonly. The father launched himself into the hallway, and Sam jumped to his own feet.

"Don't!" he yelled, but just as the father left the room, the door slammed shut once more, leaving Sam in utter blackness. He stood there, unwilling and unable to move or do anything. His heart might have stopped beating. He stopped breathing. He felt as though he were melting.

"Oh gods, oh gods, oh gods," he sobbed as the tears

finally overwhelmed him. He curled up in the chair again, trying to make himself as small as possible. Tears streamed down his face, and he rocked back and forth. The darkness pressed in on him, seeking to devour him.

Eventually, the well of tears ran out, and the sobbing ceased. Sam came back to his senses and decided that it was time to make a plan. He groped around for the father's box and found the matches, which he struck. Sam lit a candle and stood to his feet. He walked slowly around the room and re-lit all of the candles that had gone out. His ears strained listening for any sound of the father, but he heard nothing else in the house.

He stood in the center of the room and wondered what to do. He saw the box and decided to burn more incense. It filled the air with its sweet perfume, and Sam perched again on the edge of his chair.

Then both doors flew open. He turned to look at both but saw no one. At the far end of the room, a book flew off the shelf and landed on the ground with a loud crash. Then a book one shelf closer to Sam did the same. He rose to his feet as book after book crashed to the ground. It was as if an invisible person were walking toward him and casting a book aside off each shelf. He looked around for a weapon, anything to hold in his hand for a sense of control, but there was nothing. Instead, his hand went to the silver star around his neck, which he held tightly.

As if a gust of wind entered the room, dust began to swirl. It moved faster and faster and came together as if it were a small tornado. And then it began to change. The dust storm elongated, and two limbs came out as if it were a tree. But then it split at the roots in two. Sam gasped and backed away as the dust formed into the shape of a man. The dust continued to swirl, keeping the form of the dust man intact.

Its featureless face seemed to stare into Sam's soul. He kept backing up and fell with a crash as he tripped over the chair leg. He immediately jumped back to his feet and looked to the dust man, but he was gone. Then he saw movement. The dust man was mere feet from him, its arm outstretched and ready to grab him. He jumped away from the dust man and screamed. Then he ran for the other side of the room. He pulled and pushed at the door, but it would not budge. He turned in a panic and looked over his shoulder and saw the dust man advancing toward him, its right arm still held out for him. He did not know what would happen if the dust man reached him, but he knew it would not be good.

"Father Gilden!" Sam screamed at top of his lungs. "Lord Beckonly! Lady Beckonly! Anyone!" The dust man was closing in on him.

"Oh gods, oh gods," he moaned, and tears streamed down his face. He fell to his knees and cowered before the dust man. In one final moment of desperation, he threw himself sideways and began crawling away from the dust man, which continued to advance upon him. He tried to scramble back to his feet, but fear had caused him to lose all control of his body. He fell to the floor and pulled his knees to his chest. He held his hand up, as if trying to block the dust man. He sobbed harder than ever as the dust man reached down, down, down toward him. He felt the wind, he felt the small particles of dust collide with his hand, and he recoiled in even greater fear. He closed his eyes and waited for it all to end.

The seconds grew longer, and nothing had yet happened. He slowly opened one eye and saw the dust man still standing over him, but its attention was not on him. It was looking back toward the room at something that Sam could not see from where he was on the floor. But then the dust man turned back toward him and reached forward with a swirling hand. Sam screamed in terror.

"Be gone!" The strong voice of Father Gilden shook the room. The dust man froze and turned its back on Sam.

Sam took the opportunity to scurry into the corner and stood to his feet again. Father Gilden was striding toward the dust man with fire in his eyes.

"Be gone, you apparition of evil!"

The dust man seemed to gather itself and then began moving slowly towards Father Gilden. Father Gilden kept coming.

"Be gone, you foul creature!"

They were mere feet from each other now, and the dust man reached forward to grab the father by the throat.

"By the gods above, be gone!"

The dust man vanished in a cloud and for a few seconds, Sam could not see the father. Then the cloud of dust began to clear, and Father Gilden stepped through it, waving his hands to dissipate it.

"Father!" Sam cried, utterly relieved.

"Sam," the father said, smiling. "I am so happy to see you!"

Just then, the Lord Beckonly entered the room, wrapped in a robe.

"What is going on?" Lord Beckonly asked, with the impatience of someone wishing he were back in bed. "I heard screaming."

"Is Lady Beckonly awake?" Father Gilden asked, concerned.

"I don't know," Lord Beckonly said.

"It is nearly dawn," Father Gilden remarked, looking out the window at the gray mists of the early morning. "Let her sleep if she is still asleep. But sit, my Lord. There is much to discuss."

Lord Beckonly tied his robe tighter around his middle and took a seat in one of the chairs. Father Gilden gestured for Sam to sit, but he himself remained standing and began to pace back and forth in front of the window.

"What have you discovered?" Lord Beckonly asked.

"Lord Beckonly, let us be frank with one another," Father Gilden said, still pacing. "How long will you keep up this charade?"

"Charade? What charade?" Lord Beckonly asked, affronted. Sam was as confused as Lord Beckonly.

"What I mean, my Lord," Father Gilden said with extra sarcasm in his voice, "Is why did you ask us here to cast out spirits when there were not any spirits to cast out? But of course, you knew this."

"What?" Sam asked. "I don't … I don't understand. The books. The dust man!"

"Yes, those were very real things," Father Gilden said. "But they were not the work of a spirit. They were the work of a man. This man, actually. Our Lord Beckonly is a sorcerer."

The statement hung in the air like the recently dissipated dust man.

"You see, Sam," Father Gilden continued, "he does not even deny it."

A soft chuckle escaped from Lord Beckonly's lips.

"Father Gilden," he said, "I underestimated you. How did you figure it out?"

"The signs were there, to the discerning eye," Father Gilden explained. "But what interests me most is why? And I think I know."

"Have a guess," Lord Beckonly said, but the smile on his did nothing to hide the menace in his eyes.

"Gladly," Father Gilden replied. "My suspicions began on our way here. The cart tracks were deeper on the other side of the road, meaning that heavier loads were coming from this house rather than going to this house. The second thing I noticed is that a house this size should have a much larger staff than what you have here. Third, I noticed the rather well-worn look of your clothing. I also noticed that this library appears to be missing many books.

"The dust is heavy in some places, showing that it is not a well-cared for room, but the layer of dust on the shelves where there are no books is significantly thinner than the other layers of dust. This means many books have been removed recently. Taking all of these things into account, I deduce that you are broke, or on your way there. The cart tracks show that large and heavy possessions have been leaving the house, probably to be sold. Staff members have been let go to save on funds. The things being moved around the house that Lady Beckonly mentioned are actually the result of things being taken and sold off."

Sam watched the father in awe, and he had no idea how he had missed these clues. Lord Beckonly's self-assured grin was replaced by a grimace.

"I did not know the connection between your financial issues and the supernatural elements of our trip here until just a few minutes ago when you entered this room. You came in here too soon after your dust man apparition disappeared. If screams had woken you, you would have come down much earlier, and Lady Beckonly with you. But you were already awake, pulling the strings through your sorcery that have bewitched Sam and myself all evening."

"Very good, Father," Lord Beckonly said, standing to his feet. "You have caught me."

"But why?" Sam blurted out. "What do money issues have to do with the spirits—I mean, sorcery?"

"I am a proud man," Lord Beckonly said. "I did not

want my wife to discover I was a beggar. The idea for spirits came when I began selling off possessions. I started small, a necklace here, some silver there. And then I had to keep it going, so she would believe. It got out of control. I had hoped maybe to drive her off. I am not worthy to be her husband. She deserves happiness."

"She deserves a husband who will tell her the truth," Father Gilden said sternly. "By the gods, man, how could you?"

"Forgive me, Father," Lord Beckonly said, and he kneeled before the father in penance.

Just then, Lady Beckonly entered the room. Her confusion was plain upon her face.

"Lord Beckonly," Father Gilden said, "please explain to your wife."

ON THE CART ride back into town, Sam pondered all that had happened. He was bursting with questions still.

"Speak your mind, Sam," Father Gilden said, as if reading his thoughts.

"How?" Sam asked. "Just how? All of it. The cart tracks, the other clues, I don't understand."

"Open eyes and an inquisitive spirit are the recipe for noticing all sorts of wondrous and intriguing things."

"I wouldn't have even thought to make anything of the cart tracks," Sam said.

"Ah, but now you will be looking out for things like that. You are aware."

"I don't want to do anything like that for a long time," Sam replied. "Probably ever."

"If you spend time with me, you are bound to be summoned to more supernatural events."

The cart bumped and bounced along as it entered the

town and clattered down the cobblestone street. Just then, they heard a commotion of yelling and running. Father Gilden eased the cart to a halt as a woman ran up to them.

"Father, Father!" she yelled as she came near them. "You have to come quick, there are demons on the loose!"

With a twinkle in his eye, Father Gilden winked at Sam. The boy threw his head back and sighed as the father started the cart forward towards the commotion.

Dealings with the Devil

Alaine Greyson

Today was a day from hell. Trudy Cox trudged into her one-bedroom apartment and slammed the door. Her computer bag and purse fell to the floor as she sloughed onto her teal sofa. Even the comfort of the plush cushions couldn't soften the blow.

When she had woken this morning, everything had been wonderful. Her mom had been healthy, her job had been secure, and her boyfriend had been attentive and loving. Now everything had changed. She reached for the television remote and scrolled through the channels. Something mindless might dull the pain.

Trudy's purse buzzed against the bottom of the couch. *Not now.* She threw the remote on the coffee table and placed her head in her hands. It could only be one person. Trudy scrunched her eyes and tried to will the phone to stop. She didn't want to talk and relive her day. As she rocked back and forth on the couch, tears streaming down her face, the buzzing continued. Trudy stood, cupped her hands over her ears then paced the length of her small living room. Wasn't it enough that her life had crumbled this morning? Did she have to talk about and experience the pain a second time? She grasped her purse and threw it against the living room wall, her cellphone ejecting onto the floor.

Susanne. The name displayed across the screen as it continued to vibrate. Trudy had said little to her best friend —enough to spark her compassion—but Trudy kept most of the day's events to herself. After all, there was little Susanne could do or say to make things better. Nothing could take away the pain.

Trudy wiped her cheek with the back of her hand. The buzzing echoed in her brain, causing her head to throb. She approached the cellphone and denied the call. Something had to make the pain end. Trudy threw the cellphone on the floor and trudged toward the bathroom. Her life played out in her mind as she entered the tiny bathroom. The walls seemed to close around her; her mind heavy with grief. This wasn't supposed to happen. She had a good life. Her parents were supportive and loving; she had landed her dream job at as a paralegal at an important law firm; she had snagged a gorgeous lawyer and had a bevy of friends. Then she had woken up today. Trudy opened the medicine cabinet, her lip trembling as she stared.

"Well, if you're going to do it, just get it done with. No need to dither."

Trudy startled. The stress of the day had gotten to her, and now she was hearing voices. She shook her head and reached toward the cabinet.

"Have anything good in there? You need something strong if you're going to do the job right. Otherwise, you'll just end up with an upset belly."

Trudy glanced to her side. A young girl sat on the toilet, a smirk on her pale face. She was seeing and hearing things. There was no other explanation. Trudy turned toward the medicine cabinet and reached for a bottle of Tylenol.

A hand snatched the bottle from Trudy's hands. "Amateur. Tylenol? Don't you have anything stronger? Something that can take you out quick, no fooling around." The girl pushed Trudy aside and rummaged through the medicine cabinet. "Here it is. Vicodin." She shook the bottle. "Nearly full too. Wasn't this from …"

Trudy retrieved the bottle from her hands. "It's from my car accident a few months ago. Carter took good care of me, and I didn't need the pills."

"Is Carter taking good care of you now?"

Trudy scowled then turned on her heel. This figment of her imagination asked too many questions. She marched into the living room and set the pill bottle on the coffee table before she sunk into the cushions.

"So, you had a bad day. Tell me about it. Might as well get it all out before you off yourself."

"I'm not telling an imaginary person about my problems."

The girl threw the pill bottle, hitting Trudy in the face. "Then take the pills and be done with it. That's what you want, right? For the pain to end? Take them."

Trudy twirled the pill bottle in her hand. She wanted the pain to end. Taking the Vicodin would help. Then she wouldn't have to talk about her job, her mom, or Carter. It would all go away, and she would be free.

"Do you want me to open the bottle for you?"

Trudy scrunched her nose. "No. Why do you want me to take these? What's your angle? Better yet, are you real, or am I imagining you?"

The girl cackled. "What do you think? You're talking to

me. Would someone who existed only in your mind answer you?"

"Possibly. I've never imagined someone before."

"If you're imagining me, you might want to ask yourself why."

That was easy. Trudy knew why she had imagined her. Too much grief all at once had pushed her over the edge, and now she was certifiably crazy. "Tell me why I should take the pills."

"Why do you want to take them?"

The day's events played in Trudy's head. Taking the pills would be easier than reliving the pain. She placed her hand on the lid.

"Wait! What's so bad that you've come to this?"

"You snuck into my bathroom. You knew about the Vicodin. Shouldn't you know what happened? Why else are you here?"

The girl chuckled. "That's assuming I'm real."

"But, if you're not, then you know anyway, because I'm imagining you."

The girl stroked her chin and nodded. "You got me there. But seriously, tell me what happened. I'm a good listener."

Is that what she needed, a good listener? Like discussing it would somehow make everything right. Trudy sighed. "Ever have a day where everything you knew crumbled and you were left with nothing?"

"Nothing, huh? What did you lose?"

"For starters, I lost my job."

The girl approached Trudy and sat on the coffee table, meeting her gaze. "Something you did?"

"No. They said they fired me for my own good. As a push to make me go to law school."

"That sounds positive. Did you apply to law school?"

Trudy stood and strolled toward the balcony off the living room. She pulled back the curtains and gazed onto the courtyard. "Yes, but I turned it down."

"That's a boneheaded move. It sounds like your boss wanted to push you toward something better."

Trudy smirked. "So, he fired me? Now I have no income and no way to afford law school. Sounds stupid." The girl's opinion made no sense. Who got fired because their boss thought they could do better in life somewhere else? It didn't make sense.

"You led with her job issue? Lame."

Trudy jolted. A black-haired, middle-aged woman sat on a bar stool between her kitchen and living room.

"Gretchen. Why are you here? I have this."

Gretchen stood and strolled toward Trudy and the young girl. "Do you? Where's the bottle?"

The girl fixed her gaze on the floor.

"Don't have it, do you, Miranda? Why they send a young witch to do a sorceress's job …"

"Think you can do better? She's the one hellbent on killing herself. Let's see what your magic can accomplish."

Gretchen and Miranda. They had names. Trudy squeezed her eyes shut, trying to make sense of the conversation. Were they figments of her imagination, or did a witch and a sorceress crash her pity party?

Trudy flashed a hesitant smile as Gretchen approached. She clutched the pill bottle close to her chest and backed up toward the couch.

"Hello, Trudy. My wayward colleague didn't explain our presence, did she? I'm not surprised. Her generation prefers to keep people in suspense. Make them think they're dreaming or something." Gretchen positioned herself on the couch, crossing her legs and patting the cushion beside her. "Sit. It's okay. We don't bite."

Trudy stumbled past Gretchen's long legs and plunged into the cushion.

Miranda joined on the other side.

Great. Sandwiched between two magical beings. What else can go wrong today?

Gretchen leaned against the corner of the couch and folded her arms in her lap. "Had a bad day I take it?"

Trudy huffed. "Ya think?"

"Sorry about that. We wouldn't be here if everything was sunshine and roses."

Miranda shot Gretchen disparaging look. "Yeah, you're getting a lot further than I did."

Gretchen tilted her head and pursed her lips. "Pardon my young friend. She's still in training."

"I didn't know witches and sorceresses were related. How does that work?"

"Oh, it's a long tradition. We try to work together so we're not—"

Gretchen's eyes bulged. "Enough! We're not here to explain our history. We're here to help Trudy."

"Help me how?"

Gretchen eyed the pill bottle in Trudy's hand. "You desire to kill yourself, no?"

Trudy studied the bottle and twirled it in her hand. Did she want to kill herself? She wanted the pain to disappear. And downing the bottle of Vicodin would do the trick. "What if I do?"

"It's a permanent decision. We want to ensure know the consequences," Gretchen said.

"I'm pretty sure I know the consequences of killing myself."

"Do you?"

A buzzing sounded from the floor. Trudy glanced at Gretchen and Miranda then bolted toward the cellphone.

She turned it over, saw the name and threw it on the coffee table.

"Who was it?" Miranda asked

"No one of any importance." *Only my dad. Probably wondering why I wasn't at the hospital.* Trudy couldn't stand hospitals since her brief stay a few months ago when she was in a car accident, the reason for the Vicodin. They were confining and smelled of death. She didn't want to wallow in the idea that her mother—

"It was your dad, wasn't it? News about your mother? Wouldn't you want to hear that?" Gretchen grabbed the cellphone. "He left a message. Want to hear it?"

"No. I want you to go away, so I can deal with this wretched day."

"Deal? By suicide? We'll see. We're not here to prevent you but to make you understand your actions."

"I think she understands fine. Can't we just leave her? This is getting boring."

Miranda yawned and placed her head on the back of the couch.

Gretchen scowled at Miranda then approached Trudy. "Your mom is in the hospital. It wasn't expected. Something happened."

A tear welled in Trudy's eye. "Everything was perfect last night. Carter and I had dinner at my parents' house. We played cards and laughed. But this morning, I woke up in another world."

"When the unexpected occurs, it can feel like a different life. Tell me what happened." Gretchen caressed Trudy's hands and led her to the couch.

Miranda leaned forward, her elbows on her knees. "Might as well tell us what happened. Let it out."

Trudy didn't want to let it out. If she did, the tears would flow, and the pain would start. She needed to stuff her feelings deep inside where no one could reach them. "I don't know what talking about it will do. It won't fix anything. Mom is lying in that hospital bed in a coma with little hope of survival. What can I do to fix that?"

"No one asked you to fix it. But you can take steps to heal yourself. Why aren't you by her side? Doesn't your dad need you?" Gretchen asked.

He has Drew, the golden child. "My brother is there. What could I do? Pace the floor and wait for news of her passing? No thank you."

"What if your dad just had good news? You wouldn't know," Miranda said.

"She had a massive heart attack out of nowhere. The doctors weren't very hopeful." Trudy glanced at the cellphone. "I'm better off not knowing."

Miranda stood and placed her hands on her hips. "Let me get this straight. You were fired from a job because your employer thought you should go to law school. Your mom had a heart attack, but you didn't want to stay at the hospital to support your dad. And now you want to kill yourself. Are we missing something? I mean, isn't killing yourself kind of drastic, given the circumstances?"

Trudy glanced at Miranda then latched onto the coffee table as the lights flickered. A bolt of lightning struck, and the room went dark. Trudy clutched Gretchen's arm as a dark figure entered the room.

"There's your answer, Miranda. He's here."

Trudy tilted her head and wrinkled her nose. "Who's he?"

Miranda stumbled toward Gretchen and clutched her shoulders. "I hate this part. Why can't I have a mission that doesn't involve him?"

Gretchen shook her head. "He likes to stick his nose in everything." Gretchen yelled into the darkness, "Enough with the drama! We know it's you! Isn't your mere presence scary enough?"

Trudy squinted and tried to discern the figure they were talking to but to no avail. The darkness was too thick and blinded her. Who was this third visitor, and what did he want? Trudy tripped on the coffee table leg and fell backward onto the couch.

"Now, now. No need to get frightened. He thinks these antics help him convince people he has ultimate power." Gretchen cupped her hand to her mouth and whispered, "He doesn't."

Another bolt of lightning struck, accompanied by a booming voice. "Gretchen, my old friend. I didn't expect to see you tonight."

"I could say the same, Lucifer. This is a simple enough case. Your presence isn't required."

Lucifer. The Devil? The night had taken a turn for the worse. Trudy glanced at the pill bottle. Forget the rest of today. This haunting of a witch, sorceress, and now the Devil was enough to end things. No one would ever believe her if she explained.

"Whenever I see opportunity, I'm there. This is no different. Besides, I'm convinced this will be an easy sell." Lucifer nodded toward Miranda. "Sending in the young ones to do an adult's job? No worries. Just makes my sell easier."

Miranda balled her fists and pursed her lips. She stepped toward Lucifer, but Gretchen pushed her onto the couch.

"It would help if you turned the lights back on, Luce. If you want a conversation, it helps if she can see you."

Without thinking, Trudy latched onto Miranda's arm. The darkness was good enough. She didn't want to know what the Devil looked like and confirm her childhood nightmares. Trudy squeezed her eyes shut as a loud clap reverberated around the room.

Miranda elbowed Trudy in the ribs. "Open your eyes."

Trudy covered her face with her hands. "This is a dream. That means a beastlike red creature is standing in my living room. I'm good."

Miranda giggled. "Beastlike? Do you believe everything you read? Stop believing the stereotypes and open your eyes."

Trudy removed her hands from her face and blinked. Standing next to Gretchen was the handsomest man she had ever seen. His black hair fell to one side; his smile illuminated his green eyes and his dimples. The Devil had dimples. Trudy couldn't wrap her head around his appearance. Wasn't the Devil supposed to be ugly, carry a pitchfork, and have a tail?

Lucifer snapped his fingers. "It's rude to stare." He strolled toward Trudy and positioned himself on the cushion next to her. "Had a bad day, hun?"

Trudy stifled a laugh. This was too much. "You could say that."

Miranda leaned across Trudy and met Lucifer's gaze. "We already discussed her job and her mother."

"And …?"

Gretchen sighed. "We got nowhere. Something else is causing her pain."

Lucifer stroked his chin. "Losing your job and almost losing your mom wasn't enough to push you over the edge." A gleam appeared in Lucifer's eyes. "It's a boy. It's always a boy. You're dating that lawyer, Carter, right?"

Trudy scowled. "None of your business."

"Ah, my dear, but it is my business. Everything is my business. What happened? Did he break up with you?"

"I'm not discussing it, so, if the three of you would leave …"

Miranda stroked the back of her hand. "It's okay. Let it out. We're here to help."

Gretchen smirked. "*We're* here to help. I'm not too sure about Luce."

"I enjoy a good breakup story. Let's hear it. Trudy? We're waiting."

Trudy shifted her gaze from Gretchen to Lucifer. Was this a nightly thing, going around town to counsel people about their bad days? She didn't figure the Devil for the listening type. "Carter's a jerk who doesn't deserve my headspace."

"Yet you'd kill yourself over him?" Lucifer asked. "Interesting."

Trudy stood and glared at Lucifer. "You don't understand. No one understands. I lost everything today. My job, my mom, Carter."

"Technically your mom is——"

"Unless you can change things, shut up."

Lucifer bowled over in laughter. "Oh, honey, I can change things. But can you pay the price?"

The price? He meant her soul. That's what the Devil always wanted, right? He walked the Earth, collecting souls, and now he wanted hers.

"Don't listen to him. This isn't worth your soul. Do you really want to spend the afterlife with him? He may be nice to look at but——"

"You flatter me, Gretchen." Lucifer reached for Trudy's hands. "Look, honey. You want your job back, your mom healthy, and this Carter guy to love you again?"

That's what she wanted, right? Miranda and Gretchen wanted to talk, but Lucifer, he could actually do something about her mess. She could get her life back, and all it would cost was her soul. That's not so bad, especially since she didn't believe in the afterlife. And, if she didn't believe, what would it really cost her? She reached her hand toward Lucifer.

Miranda jumped between them. "Stop." She glared at Lucifer. "You know the rules. She hasn't dealt with her feelings about Carter yet. You can't make a deal until she's had a chance to release her pain."

Lucifer sighed and sank into the cushion. "Fine. Tell us about lover boy. But spare me the mushy stuff."

"What's to tell? Last night, we were a couple, and this morning, after I lost my job and my mom had a heart attack, he told me he was in love with this girl from the gym. He knew I was having a bad day, yet he still thought that was the time to tell me. Is that enough?"

Gretchen wrapped her arms around Trudy's shoulders. "I'm so sorry that happened." She scowled at Lucifer. "Men are assholes."

Sniffing back a tear, Trudy turned and placed her head on Gretchen's chest. "I don't understand what happened. He said he wouldn't break my heart. He promised he would never leave. But, when I was at my lowest, when everything crumbled, he vanished. I can't process that." She clutched the pill bottle. "What do I have left?"

"He's gone, and he's not coming back. But that doesn't mean your life has to end. No one is worth killing yourself over. You have worth and a future. Block him, get him out of your life and move on," Gretchen said.

"But he was it. He was the one. No one compares." Tears streaked Trudy's face as her hand wrapped around the pill bottle. "I can't go on without him. He was my everything, and now what do I have? Loneliness, bitterness, a broken heart. That's no way to live." She opened the lid.

Everything turned black. A loud voice echoed in

Trudy's ears, followed by screaming and crying. Where was she? She fought the pounding in her head and forced her eyes open. EMTs and a few firefighters buzzed around her. She searched for Lucifer and Gretchen but couldn't find them. Her hand scoured the floor and enveloped an empty pill bottle. Had she taken the pills?

"Trudy, I'm so glad you're okay. You scared me! Next time, talk things out with me, okay?" Susanne wiped away a tear. "What am I saying? There won't be a next time. We'll get through this, I promise. I'm not leaving you."

Trudy nodded then glanced toward the kitchen.

Miranda sat cross-legged on the island and smiled.

Whatever happened with Lucifer, it was done. And now Trudy could move on. She adjusted herself on the stretcher when an EMT approached.

He leaned over, his black hair falling to one side, illuminating his green eyes and dimples. *Dimples.*

"Hello, Trudy. My name is Lucien, and I promise to take very good care of you."

Trudy glanced toward the kitchen, but Miranda was no longer there. She inhaled and flashed Lucien an uneasy smile. What had she done?

Vandalized by Darkness

Marie McGrath

"Jesse Jensen!"

"What Billie? For god's sake, I'm busy!" Jesse shouted.

"Those little brats are in our yard, *again*. I'm exhausted with constantly picking up the trash." Billie sighed and frowned. "I get that it's October and pranks are *fun*, but seriously, this place is not a dumping ground."

Jesse walked from the back of the house; his body glistened with sweat. He wiped his brow with the back of his hand and patted his hands on his jeans.

Billie whistled. *My husband is gorgeous.*

"Billie, I understand you're frustrated, but they're young and stupid. You know how we were. Hell, still are! We're only in our twenties. When did you shove a stick up your ass and get all crotchety?"

Billie crossed her arms. "When our house is constantly vandalized! I'm tired of this. I clean the toilet paper off our trees and pick garbage from the grass, and yet, every morning, it's a *mess* again!"

Jesse closed the gap between them and wrapped his

arms around her. He kissed her neck and nibbled up to her ear. "Just relax. Okay? I'll take care of it."

Billie's shoulders slumped, and she leaned against him. He always knew how to center her again. No matter what. It was one of the reasons they had fallen in love so quickly and so young.

Billie faced Jesse and peered into his eyes. "You promise?"

He leaned in and kissed the tip of her nose. "Promise."

She bit the corner of her lip as she brushed her fingertips across his chest. His abs rippled under his skin— taut and tantalizing.

Jesse smiled a devilish grin, his gray eyes sparkling in that mischievous way.

"What?"

Jesse winked then whisked her off her feet.

She yelped in surprise then broke out into a hearty laugh. This was the man she loved. This was the man who made everything better—something she never wanted to forget.

BILLIE STARTLED. She fell asleep after Jesse had whisked her to their bedroom. She rubbed her forehead. The tension behind her temples wouldn't ease. She stood and peered through the bedroom window. It was dark. Had she really napped that long?

She fixed the curtains and trudged down the stairs. "Jesse? Where are you?" She checked every room but heard nothing. Where on earth would he be at this hour? And why hadn't he told her where he was going?

She looked outside in his garage, but again, it was

vacant. She squeezed the bridge of her nose. Where was he, and why did her head throb so much?

The front yard was the only place she hadn't checked. Maybe he was finally taking care of all the destruction. She peered around the side of the house with a direct view of the front yard. She huffed. *These kids are ridiculous. Why can't they stay out of my yard?*

The trash was everywhere. Shingles were scattered all around, shutters hanging off the hinges, beer cans and bottles were littered everywhere she looked. "What the hell?" she muttered. How could the yard possibly be worse from this morning? It made no sense. She walked to the edge of the yard and peered down the street.

Someone with a red hoodie pulled tight around their face and wearing jeans was hiding behind a tree across the road.

"Hey, you!" She tried to move closer but stopped. "What are you doing over there? Did you do all of this?" She grabbed a discarded can and threw it at the tree. "Stay out of my yard. You hear me?"

They didn't move and stood as still as possible.

Billie trudged back to her front door, waving her hands in the air, and practically growled. Nothing made sense anymore, and her headache hurt too much. She plopped on the sofa as her eyelids fluttered close.

Jesse would hear about this and so would the kids once she rested a little more.

JESSE KICKED the fourth beer can he found in the yard. It was one thing to treat the yard as a dump, it was another to do it and not share any of the beer. He chuckled. He wouldn't have cared the first time the kids fooled around in his yard, but this was absurd.

He needed to do something. Billie wouldn't stop complaining about it, and he could see her point, but the kids were persistent. He needed to catch them and rat out those little shit friends of theirs.

Jesse's face beamed. He knew exactly what to do. A trip to the store and he would have some cameras set up around the house. It was perfect.

He walked to the garage and sat in his car. He turned the key, but nothing happened. He turned it again and listened for some kind of noise, but there was only silence. He slammed his hand against the steering wheel. Why couldn't anything go right lately? If he couldn't drive to the store to get cameras, he would walk. Town wasn't that far.

"Billie, I'm headed to the store! I'll be back later," he shouted.

Jesse shook his head. Billie was isolating herself more lately, taking *naps* and drifting off. Jesse pulled the front door shut and locked it. He walked around the beer bottles and rusted bike parts to the sidewalk.

He halted as a group of teenagers snuck toward him. They couldn't possibly be the ones trespassing and vandalizing the property, could they?

He ducked behind a bush at the side and waited. He wanted to catch them in the act and scare some sense into them.

The teenage boys stood in a circle at the edge of Jesse's property. They held something shiny, but Jesse wasn't sure what it was.

"Brett, you're such a wuss. Just do it already, so we can go."

"I *will* do it!"

Brett was the shortest in the group, with reddish brown hair and freckles all over his face.

Jesse tensed. What exactly was *Brett* supposed to do?

The boy grabbed a large rock then tossed it around in his hands. The other boys pushed him, and he groaned. He reached back his arm and launched the rock at the front window.

Jesse watched the rock as if it moved in slow motion. *They came to throw rocks at my house?* Jesse jumped to his feet and bolted toward the boys. "What the hell do you think you all are doing?" Jesse's ears echoed with the sound of shattered glass.

"Let's get out of here!" the boys shouted.

"Don't you leave. You broke my window!"

Brett's hands shook as he stared at the scene. Jesse was inches from grabbing Brett's shirt when he turned and ran. Jesse tried to catch him, but he disappeared too fast.

"Well, shit," Jesse said. What had happened? How did those kids get away? He had been so close, and yet, it didn't matter. He ran his fingers through his hair. Billie would go ballistic if she saw the window. He had to clean it up before she saw. There was nothing else to do.

BILLIE STARTLED at the sound of glass shattering. What in the world happened? She leapt off the sofa in time to see a rock land on the floor in the foyer. She screamed at the sight.

Jesse bounded through the front door. "It's okay. I'm taking care of it."

Billie crossed her arms. "Taking care of what, exactly?"

"Nothing. Just a little mishap, is all."

Her eyebrows drew together. "You call a rock through our window a *little mishap?*"

Jesse wrung his hands. "Okay, maybe a little more, but I have it handled."

"Do you care to explain how it got through our window?"

Jesse shoved his hands in his pants' pockets. "The neighbors?"

Billie screamed, "*Again?* When is this going to end? I'm tired of it."

Jesse moved closer to her and put his hands on her shoulders. "I know, but I scared them away."

"You saw them?"

Jesse nodded.

"Fine. But if they do *anything* else, I'm going to let you all have it. This is getting absurd. I can't live like this, and I refuse to accept it." Billie stomped up the stairs. Jesse could take care of the mess himself. It served him right for not doing more about it anyway. *Who sees the perpetrators and does nothing about it? He scared them away? What does that even mean?* She plopped on their bed and turned on music, letting the sound soothe her.

JESSE CURSED UNDER HIS BREATH. He understood Billie was under a lot of stress with the vandalism but to take it out on him? That was too much. He couldn't control the kids from destroying their house. It wasn't like he opened the door and said, *"Go ahead. Smash it all up. Litter in my yard. No problem."* He was pissed about it all too.

He found the broom and swept up the shards. Luckily, it wasn't a large window, or the mess would have been much worse. Finally, when all the pieces were swept up,

Jesse grabbed a beer from the refrigerator. He popped the top and walked to the sofa. This day had been exhausting; he needed to take the edge off.

He turned the TV to the sports network. The more he watched, the more he noticed the picture messed up. Every once and awhile, lines would run vertically through the picture then clear up. Jesse approached the TV and smacked it. The picture cleared. Satisfied, he sat back on the couch.

Halfway through the football game, Billie returned downstairs.

"Hey, honey," Jesse said.

Billie nodded. "I see you've cleaned the mess."

"Yep, all done."

"What's for dinner?"

Jesse's right eyebrow rose above the left. "I have a few ideas."

Billie shoved his shoulder. "Get real."

He wiggled his eyebrows up and down. "I am."

Billie stifled a laugh. "Well, I need real food. I can't remember the last time I ate. All this commotion has me distracted." She turned for the kitchen.

Jesse returned to the TV.

"Ugh!" she hollered.

He set the remote on the table and followed the noise. "What's wrong?"

"You didn't stock the fridge. We have no food."

"No worries. We can do takeout."

She crossed her arms. "I don't want takeout. I'm watching my weight. You know … to fit into my costume."

Jesse rolled his eyes. "You look great, babe."

"You have to say that. You're my husband."

"Well, actually, I don't. And I do think you look great. I can run to the store if you want."

She shook her head. "No, it's fine. I'll just go to bed."

"You sure? You just said you needed food."

She shrugged. "I'm not hungry anymore."

"If you're sure."

She nodded then kissed his forehead. "Goodnight. Don't stay up too late watching TV."

"I won't. Night."

Jesse watched Billie walk up the stairs then refocused on the TV. He didn't understand her. Who said they needed food then went to bed? Something was seriously up with her, and he had no idea how to figure it out.

DAYLIGHT STREAMED THROUGH THE WINDOW. Billie rolled to her side to see Jesse's side of the bed empty. She rubbed her eyes and stretched. A headache brewed just at the edges. She balled her fists. "No. Not again."

She willed her mind to stop throbbing. It actually kind of helped. She walked downstairs and into the kitchen. She had hoped Jesse would be there, but he didn't seem to be anywhere. She shrugged. She was determined to have a better day. Things didn't feel like they used to anymore, and she would force it if she had to. *Mind over matter, Billie. Mind over matter.*

She walked to the French doors leading to the backyard. She peered through the door to survey the yard. The large maple trees that provided shade in the summer were losing their leaves. It was time to rake them. She rolled up her sleeves and got to work.

She heard a whistle and stopped.

"Mm-hmm, you look sexy out here, babe."

Billie wiped the sweat from her brow. "If you mean a sweaty mess, then sure."

Jesse chuckled. "Never." He walked to her and forced the rake from her hand. He grabbed both hands and danced her around the piles of leaves.

She relaxed into his arms and smiled.

They stopped, and he twirled her. At the last spin, they launched into the largest pile of leaves, laughed and stared skyward.

Billie raised Jesse's hand to her lips and gently kissed him. "Thanks. I needed that."

He smiled. "Me too." He tucked a stray hair behind her ear. "I meant what I said earlier. You look beautiful."

She smiled. "Well, thanks. Wanna help?"

"I wouldn't want to do anything else." Jesse jumped to his feet then outstretched his hand to help Billie up. He grabbed the rake from the ground and raked the leaves they had dispersed in their fun.

Billie grabbed garbage bags and loaded the leaves, leaving a nice and tidy yard.

"TODAY'S BEEN A GREAT DAY," Billie said.

Jesse nodded as he entwined their bodies in a hug. "I couldn't agree more."

"Want to watch a movie?"

"Sure. I'll set it up."

"And I'll see if I can scrounge some snacks."

Jesse headed toward the TV while Billie went to the kitchen. Billie waited and watched as Jesse fiddled with the TV. He found a movie and sat on the couch. Billie spread across the sofa and laid her head in his lap.

Jesse bent and kissed her before he focused on the movie.

The TV picture went dark.

"What the …?" Jesse said.

"What happened?"

Jesse shook his head. "Not sure. Can you turn on the light? Maybe a cord is loose."

Billie nodded and went to the light switch. She flipped it up, and nothing happened. After a few more times, she stopped. "The lights are out too."

Jesse ran his hands through his hair. "Can nothing ever go right?"

Billie crossed her arms. "Did you pay the electric bill?"

"What? Of course, I did."

Billie narrowed her gaze. "Are you sure? As a matter of fact, have you even been working lately? You're always in that garage of yours, but I never see you dressed for work."

"How can you say that? I've been working. Why would I shirk my responsibilities?"

"Hmm, let's see. Because that's your pattern, Jesse."

Jesse raised his hands in defense. "Woah, woah, woah. How did I get put on the chopping block? Whatever is happening in this house is not my fault. I go to work." He rubbed his forehead. "I think …"

"You *think*? That's real comforting, Jesse. You *think* you go to work. I can't believe how irresponsible you are. Who just forgets to go to work and pay the bills? What else did you forget to pay? The mortgage? Insurance?" Billie huffed. "I'm tired of this. The neighbors are declaring war on our house, and my own husband can't do simple things. Figure out your shit, or I'm gone." She stomped up the stairs to leave Jesse to deal with the situation.

What had he been thinking? What had happened to them? This wasn't how they were. They squabbled occasionally but nothing like this. All this anger had seemed to surface lately. She wasn't sure where it came from, but just like the constant pounding in her head, the anger was always there just below the surface.

BILLIE'S EYES FLEW OPEN. She felt disoriented. She surveyed the room and realized she was in bed, covered in sweat. She slowly peeled her pajama shirt off her body and shook it to air out everything. Her head fell into her hands. What had she dreamt? The images seemed to float in front of her eyes.

A man in a ski mask.

Blood everywhere.

And then darkness.

She rubbed her face and forced away the fog. What was that all about? She never dreamt of death like that. Her hands shook.

Jesse was by her side before she even realized he was in the same room. "What's wrong?"

"I-I had a terrible dream." She rubbed her temples. "Something about it I can't let go."

Jesse wrapped Billie in a long embrace. "I've got you. You're safe. You're with me."

She nodded into his chest. "It just … I don't know."

He ran his hands through her hair over and over. "I've got you."

She nodded and blinked away the tears. "Okay, I'm sorry."

"Nothing to be sorry about. It was just a dream." Jesse pulled Billie to her feet. "Let's go downstairs. Relax out in the backyard, drink a beer."

She nodded and followed Jesse down the stairs. She felt calmer but still shaken from that dream. She couldn't quite put her finger on it, but something was different about the whole thing. It didn't make sense. What was the purpose? Her dreams were usually easy to decipher, but this one was different.

They walked into the backyard. Jesse had brought two beers and passed one to her. Beer wasn't her first choice, but any alcohol was well welcomed at this point. She wanted to forget about the dream and move on. The weight on her shoulders felt unbearable. Why couldn't things feel lighter and easier like they used to?

"Thanks," she whispered. "I know I haven't been the easiest to live with lately."

"Stop. It's fine."

Billie shook her head. "No. It's not. I've been awful to you lately, and I don't know why. It's not fair to you."

Jesse entwined their fingers. "I'm not going anywhere."

Billie smiled weakly and kissed Jesse's knuckles.

A door slam startled them both.

"What in the …" Jesse said.

"Who?"

Jesse raised his finger to his lips. "Stay quiet and behind me."

Billie nodded and followed him to the source of the sound.

At the front door stood two people, one in a red hoodie and one in a black hoodie.

Billie squinted toward the intruder. "Wait a minute. That's who was lurking outside behind a tree."

Jesse turned to Billie. "You've seen this person before?"

She nodded.

"Well, these aren't the guys who threw the rock in the window." Jesse approached the person wearing the red hoodie, jeans, and black sneakers. "What are you doing at my house?"

The person lowered the red hood and revealed a young

teenage girl with brown hair, freckles, and glasses. "Lower your hoodie."

The other person lowered their black hood. "Why? What's going on?"

Jesse stared at the two teens. "What's going on?" he mimicked. He looked to Billie then to the teens. "Are they serious?"

"Get away from our house!" Billie screamed.

The girl in the red hoodie raised her hands palms out in defense. "We don't mean any harm."

The girl in the black hoodie moved behind and whispered, "What are you saying?"

Billie put her hands on her hips. "Can someone explain what is happening? I asked you to leave. You're trespassing on private property. I'm calling the police."

"Wait. Please don't," the girl with the red hoodie said.

"Watch me." Billie turned.

"You don't understand. You can't do that," the girl with the red hoodie replied. "My name is Alyssa. Please, can we just talk about this?"

Jesse narrowed his gaze. "Why should we? My wife told you to get the hell out of here."

The girl in the black hoodie cowered behind Alyssa, tugging her sleeve. "Alyssa, please, can we just leave?"

Alyssa shook her head. "I can't until they know."

Jesse and Billie exchanged glances.

"Know what?" Jesse asked.

What was happening? Billie shook as she stared at these two random strangers. They didn't seem intimidating, but she couldn't fight back the feeling that something was wrong, and she wasn't sure she really wanted to know why.

"Are you sure we can't go inside and sit?" Alyssa asked.

Jesse shook his head. "Hell no. Why would I let you into my home? You two are lucky you're even here as it is."

Alyssa nodded.

Alyssa's friend tightly wrapped her arms around herself. Her gaze darted all over the room but never made eye contact with Billie or Jesse.

"Well, get on with it. I don't have all day," Jesse said.

Alyssa stepped forward then retreated. "Well, this isn't easy to tell you both. I want to make sure to say it the right way."

Billie wrung her hands. "I can't take this. Have you been vandalizing our house?"

Alyssa shook her head. "No, but what do you remember about that?"

Billie cocked her head. What did that even mean?

"What kind of question is that?" Jesse asked.

"Have you seen it happen? Do you recall the times it happens?"

"Of course, we see it happen. Our yard is constantly destroyed. We clean it up, then it's back to dump levels again every day."

"Don't you find it odd how quickly your yard is destroyed again?" Alyssa asked.

Jesse shrugged.

"Are you saying it doesn't happen every night?" Billie asked.

"For the time you have lived here, has it ever been that frequent before?"

"Well, no."

"Okay. Is there anything else you've noticed lately?"

Jesse rubbed his head. "What's your point? Cut the crap."

Alyssa crossed her arms. "Maybe it's not that people

vandalize the yard every night and more likely you don't ever clean it."

Billie knitted her brows. "What does that mean? I've cleaned it every single time. It takes forever, then it comes back tenfold the next time."

Alyssa moved closer to Billie and away from her friend. Her friend reached for her but didn't get any closer. The girl's face was pale. "Think really hard about every time you've cleaned it. Try to remember every detail you can."

Billie closed her eyes and thought hard. What did Alyssa expect her to remember? She would collect the cans and throw them in the trash. She remembered adjusting the shutters—then her vision flashed. She saw the shutters not actually moving when she tried. She shook her head. No, she moved them. She knew she had moved them.

"You haven't been able to clean up anything. Have you?" Alyssa asked.

Jesse balled his fists. "Yes, we have. We raked the yard the other day. We've cleaned the mess from the rock going through the window. That's plenty."

"You mean this mess?" Alyssa pushed Jesse out of the way, opened the front door and shuffled her feet across the foyer floor.

Billie stared at the floor, and her vision shifted from a perfectly pristine floor, to shattered glass, back to pristine. "What the …?"

Jesse stared at the floor as well. "No. I cleaned that up. I used the broom and put it in the trash."

"I'm sorry to tell you both this, but you really didn't. And sure, people have been lurking around the house and throwing stuff, but it's not every night, and it certainly hasn't been cleaned up." She paused. "Take a better look around this house. No lights. No heat. It's a mess."

Billie crossed her arms. "Jesse forgot to pay the electric bill. It's no big deal. We don't have a messy house."

"Okay. When was the last time you two went to work? Or ate?"

"Uh …" Jesse said.

"Things have been tight. That's all."

Alyssa moved even closer. "I'm sorry to be blunt, but you two aren't getting it." She sighed. "You're dead."

Dead? Had she heard Alyssa right? She wasn't dead. Dead people couldn't have done what they did. They were alive. Things were just tough.

Jesse ran his hands through his hair and stared into Billie's eyes.

"No. We-We can't be dead!" Billie shouted.

"Think about it. Do you just end up in different places and not remember where you were? Does time pass differently? Do you have feelings you just can't explain?"

"Billie, your headaches."

"You can't be serious, Jesse. You don't believe her, do you?"

Alyssa turned to her friend and whispered.

"What did you tell her?" Billie asked.

"She can't hear or see you. Only I can. I wanted her here as moral support for me, but look at her. Has she made eye contact with you? Does she react like two people are standing in front of her? She doesn't seem like it to me."

"That doesn't prove anything," Jesse said. "We're talking to you. You're alive."

Billie cradled her head in her hands. "This is all insane. I would know if I was dead." She walked a few steps away. "I need some air."

Alyssa nodded.

Billie walked to the backyard and was bombarded by

all the leaves that awaited her. She stopped dead. The leaves had been raked. They put them in the bags. What had happened?

Jesse followed her out. "This is nuts."

Billie nodded. "We would know if we were dead. Right? I mean, how would we be together?"

Jesse chuckled. "Exactly. Ghosts can't touch things, and we have. We've touched each other. This is crazy."

Billie stared at Jesse. "But we haven't eaten. I mean, I haven't. Have you?"

"No, but we had the beers. Ghosts can't do that, can they?"

Billie shrugged. "I don't know."

"Let's go back and tell Alyssa to leave. She's the crazy one."

Billie nodded.

Alyssa was alone when they both returned.

"We want you to leave," Jesse said.

"I didn't want to have to show you this, but you leave me no choice. The denial you both carry is impressive. More so than other ghosts I've met." Alyssa ruffled in her hoodie and removed a newspaper clipping. She held it in front of both Billie and Jesse. The heading read, *Couple Murdered in Their Beds*.

Billie read the article, and her eyes blurred. This couldn't be happening. Their names were in black and white. How could she deny that? The room spun, and her vision flashed. The dream that had shaken her returned in full force.

She startled, and someone in all black stood over her. She lay in bed, and all she saw was a masked individual. Her hands got clammy, and she sensed Jesse's sleeping body next to her. Her blood went cold, then a bullet flew from the gun in front of her face. The impact hit her head, and the pain exploded for a second until it was silenced by deep, dark blackness. The blackness overtook her senses. Billie coughed and swayed as the memory ended. "What … What was that?"

Jesse stared at Billie. "What happened?"

"I-I saw the gunman. He came into our house and into our bedroom and shot me. Then everything went black."

Alyssa nodded.

"Is that why I feel the headaches? And the anger?"

"I can't explain the symptoms you have. It's different for everyone. But I imagine the tragic way you both died has kept you from moving on, especially with how thick your denial was."

This couldn't be happening. How could they be dead? They had barely lived. The thought took away Billie's breath.

"Why can't I remember?" Jesse whispered.

"I-I think you were asleep, babe. I didn't see you move."

Jesse ran his hands through his hair. "What now? What happens next?"

Alyssa shrugged. "I can't answer that. Your options are to move on or to stay here and be stuck."

"And if we move on?" Billie asked.

"I don't know what happens there either. I do know that by staying here, you'll continue to lose yourselves. You'll get angrier. It doesn't end nicely."

Billie moved to Jesse. "What do you think? What should we do?"

Jesse shrugged.

Tears fell down Billie's cheeks. How could this be possible? How could her life have been stolen from her? From them?

"This isn't fair," Billie said.

Jesse wrapped his arms around Billie the best he could. It wasn't the same now that they knew, but it would have to do. "I love you, Billie Jensen. Even in death we stayed together. Wherever we go, as long as I'm with you, I don't care."

Billie nodded. "How do we do it?"

"Focus on the peace, and let it overwhelm you. Then let go of this life, and you'll move on."

They both nodded and closed their eyes. The peace Alyssa mentioned felt strange, but it had been there, buried deep. She focused on the feeling and let it consume her— until all she knew was peace.

She opened her eyes just as Jesse did the same. They stared lovingly at each other until everything faded. Overwhelmed by the peace, they both let go.

Possession Obsession

Alaine Greyson

Dreams can come true, until those dreams turn into nightmares—a concept Lewis Thompson knew too well. Today was his first day back at the office after a long hiatus. And his boss expected him at full capacity, not skipping a beat. Lewis pulled on his suit jacket and reached for his briefcase. His first day promised to be long and full of meetings about his company's latest merger. The emails had poured in during his time off, but Lewis barely read them. He spent last night trying to get caught up, but his focus was not on work. How could it be? Drinking a beer on the beach sounded more comforting than the blast of demands he would likely get at the office. Three weeks off wasn't enough time, and Lewis wished he could go on a permanent vacation.

As he bent to retrieve his briefcase, Lewis glanced at the photograph on his nightstand. *Carrie.* Her blond hair and sunny smile stared back at him. A lump caught in his throat. The month prior, she had been here, with her hair tousled as she lay in bed, wishing him a good day. He leaned over and kissed the picture, like he would have done if she were present. But she wasn't. A drunk driver four weeks ago had taken care of that.

The world had frozen, and Lewis didn't want to return to the busy life he'd had before Carrie's accident. In his mind, the world stopped the day she had died. And he had spent the last three weeks hiding from family, friends, and responsibility.

Lewis straightened his tie and tightened his grasp on his briefcase. He had to eventually face people, and today was as good as any. If he kept his head down and his mouth closed, he could return to his apartment and drown himself in beer and vapid television shows. Until then, he had to plaster a smile and endure.

The glare of the summer sun shone on him as he exited his apartment building. Lewis shielded his eyes and trudged toward his silver Honda Accord. His car screamed *middle management*, something he had tried to climb up from, but Carrie's death destroyed his ambition. If he didn't have a wife or family to provide for, did it really matter how he received his paycheck? At this point, life was all about survival.

The twenty-minute drive to the office flew by and gave Lewis little time to prepare his reactions. People were bound to ask questions, offer condolences, and stare at him with those fake-pouting faces. No one had bothered to call, email, or check up on him while he grieved the past three weeks. Why should he believe they care now?

Lewis drew a breath as he exited his vehicle and grabbed his briefcase from the back seat. Tagget and Associates had owned the business center in the middle of Kingston for the past twenty years. Today, it changed hands.

As Lewis gazed at the brick façade that housed multiple businesses, from a hair salon to a pizza place to the construction company he used to call home. A hand clapped him on the back and jolted him.

"Lewis! First day back, huh? What a day to get thrown back to work." Noah Brewster, a tall, slight man with horned glasses squeezed Lewis's shoulders. Noah leaned in and whispered, "The merger has some people scared. But not me." Noah glanced around and leaned closer. "Johnson and Sons brought some hot chicks. Hot, I'm telling you." He nudged Lewis with his elbow and winked. "You're single now. I'll introduce you to Calla. Smokin'."

Lewis closed his eyes and exhaled. Carrie had only been gone a month, and Noah thought he needed to start dating? The clueless factor boggled Lewis's mind. He wrenched free from Noah's grasp and marched through the front door. This day couldn't end soon enough.

The atmosphere in the office was mixed. Some people had their heads down, hard at work, and most likely job scared. Some were mingling with the new associates, and some were ogling the hot chicks Noah had referenced. In another field, it wouldn't be uncommon for good-looking women to populate an office. But, in construction, even the office side was heavily male. After seeing Noah's reaction and the ogling of some of the men, Lewis knew why.

"That one over there, that's Calla. She's the new sales rep." Noah's breath tingled on Lewis's neck as the smell of onion wafted across his nose.

"You do know that women are people too and deserve respect, don't you?"

Noah grinned and waved at Calla. "Oh, I respect them."

Lewis rolled his eyes as Noah waltzed toward a tall brunette in the corner. He didn't understand why men like Noah weren't concerned about a harassment accusation or lawsuit. But whatever occurred would be on them. Lewis had enough on his mind. He strolled toward his cubicle and placed his briefcase on his desk.

A confident voice sounded behind him, startling him. Lewis turned and faced the tall brunette with billowy hair and a contagious smile. Did Noah send her over?

"I'm sorry. I didn't mean to frighten you." She proffered her hand. "I'm Calla, and you are?"

Lewis outstretched his hand. Her grasp was strong for a woman. Was that something he was allowed to think. Great, now he was thinking like Noah and the rest of the cavemen class. "I'm Lewis. You're new here?"

"I was going to ask the same of you." Calla flashed a wide grin.

"Nope, not new. Just back from a three-week break."

Calla tilted her head. "Vacation?"

Lewis wished. How could he tell someone he had been on leave grieving his deceased girlfriend? It didn't sound like lively conversation. "Not exactly."

Calla shook her head. "Look at me, prying. It's not my business. Whatever kept you away, welcome back. I hope this merger didn't throw you off balance."

"As long as I have a job and a paycheck, it's all good."

"We didn't buy Tagget and Associates to lay off employees. We bought it to help make it better."

Lewis scrunched his nose. "We?"

Calla held her hands to the side. "Johnson and Sons? Well, I'm one of the sons."

Whoever this Johnson was, he sounded just as sexist as the other men in the company. Who considered their daughter as one of the sons? Unless …

"I know. Some people think it's sexist. But it's okay. My dad isn't like the other Neanderthals in this office. When I joined the company, he wanted to rename it, but it has been Johnson and Sons for generations, so …"

Lewis shrugged. "As long as you're okay with it."

Calla reached over Lewis and latched onto a picture on his desk. "Cute. Girlfriend?"

Without thinking, Lewis snatched the picture and placed it back on his desk.

"Sorry. I'll leave you alone to get acclimated."

Lewis inhaled and bit his lip. "Calla, wait. That wasn't welcoming. I reacted that way for a reason. The picture, it's my girlfriend Carrie. A drunk driver killed her a month ago. That's the reason I was on leave."

Calla placed her hand on his shoulder and gazed into his eyes. "I'm so sorry. I didn't know. You have my condolences, Lewis."

"I've had condolences the past few weeks. They might mean well, but they don't take away the pain. They don't bring her back."

"I can't imagine what you're feeling, but I want to make your return easier. How about we have lunch today, and I can personally catch you up on the changes in the company? And, if you want, you can tell me about Carrie. I'm a good listener."

Lunch and talk about Carrie, was that a good idea? Lewis wasn't sure, but how could he decline his new boss's daughter? He nodded. Since Carrie's death, he had no one to talk to and release his pent-up emotions. Talking to a stranger could help. Nothing else had helped so far.

LEWIS DROVE to work the next morning with a smile on his face. His usual morning routine—waking up, getting dressed and kissing Carrie's picture—unchanged. But something was different. *Calla.* He recalled the lunch from the previous day. Calla was smart, funny, and a bit sassy.

All traits Carrie had possessed. And she had listened to him without judging, something only Carrie had done. He missed that human connection from someone who sought to understand, not deceive, and use for their own devices. It gave him something to look forward to instead of dreading the monotony.

As Lewis neared the office, a doubting voice echoed in his head. *What about Carrie?* He drew a breath. Calla was a new friend. There was nothing romantic, no attraction on either side. He needed someone to talk to, and she had offered. Nothing to feel guilty about, right? He shook his head and pulled into a parking spot.

Lewis approached the door and gazed at his hand. Why was it shaking? And why did his heart rate increase? He could feel it pounding against his chest. It didn't make sense. Work had never made him nervous before. He pushed his thoughts aside and swung open the door.

Scanning the office floor, he dodged the office gossip, Noah, and a few others who wanted to talk and marched toward his cubicle. He placed his briefcase on the floor and rifled through the stack of papers on his desk. Work had piled up, and he would have to focus today.

A husky voice whispered in his ear, "Hello, Lewis."

He jumped, his papers flying in the air.

A blonde woman bent over, collecting the wayward stack. "I have to stop scaring you like that. So sorry." She handed Lewis the papers.

He tilted his head and scrunched his eyes. "Calla?"

Calla ran her fingers through her hair and smiled. "Like it? I decided I need a change. You like blond hair, don't you?"

Lewis deposited the papers on his desk and faced Calla. He did like blond hair, mainly because Carrie was blonde, like a ray of sun. And now Calla stood before him, sunny-blond hair and a beckoning smile.

Calla pouted. "You don't like it."

"No, no. It's not that. It's just … unexpected."

"Well, I'm not the predictable type." Calla gazed toward Lewis's desk. "Carrie, what did she do for fun?"

Lewis ran his fingers over the frame. Carrie stared back, her confident smile radiating from the picture in her favorite pink and white dress. Lewis loved that dress. White piping on the sleeves and the hem with white polka dots covering the pink background—Lewis thought she looked like an angel. *That's the dress you buried her in.* Lewis glanced at Calla. She was the first person interested in Carrie. While part of him wondered why she was interested, the other part was glad someone cared. "She loved to crochet. One Christmas, she crocheted a scarf for me. It wasn't her best effort, but she tried. And she loved to cook. Italian food was her specialty."

"Sounds nice." Calla glanced toward the far end of the office. "How about dinner tonight? Your place, but I'll bring the food."

Dinner at my place? We've just met. Was this moving too fast? Lewis tried to find words.

"I don't bite. It's just a way to continue getting to know each other without all the pressures of being in public. I won't disappoint."

Lewis nodded and scratched his address on a piece of paper.

"Great! I'll let you get to work. See you tonight, handsome."

He watched Calla waltz away, wondering if he had made a mistake. His gaze rested on the picture of Carrie, and he gulped. It wasn't a date. Just two friends. And he needed a friend right now. What could go wrong?

THE DOORBELL RANG at six o'clock on the dot. Lewis glanced in the mirror then at the picture beside his bed. What would Carrie say if she knew Calla was coming to dinner? He reminded himself it was two friends hanging out, nothing more. Carrie would understand.

Lewis went to the door, surprised at his sweating palms and increasing heartbeat. If it wasn't a date, why was he nervous? He closed his eyes and swung open the door. Everything would be okay.

"Hey, Lewis! I have everything we need for a fabulous Italian dinner in my picnic basket. Isn't it cute?" Calla smiled and breezed past the doorway.

Lewis's breath hitched.

Calla strolled toward the kitchen, her blond hair flowing down her back, wearing a pink dress with white piping and white polka dots.

He swallowed hard and followed her, an uneasy feeling in his stomach.

"Stuffed shells sound good?" Calla pulled sauce, a bag of stuffed shells, and a loaf of garlic bread from the basket. She marched around the kitchen like it was her second home, gathering her supplies and preheating the oven. "You do like stuffed shells, don't you, Lewy?"

Lewis blindly reached for the bar stool, not willing to take his eyes off Calla. She had dyed her hair, now wore the same dress Carrie had in the picture in his office and was making his favorite meal and had called him *Lewy*. His imagination was off the rails. This couldn't be happening, could it?

"Be a dear, Lewy, and open the wine bottle in the basket? I like to sip on it while I cook." Calla's dress swished as she arranged the saucepan and placed a cutting board on the island. "And cut the garlic bread? You're better at it than me. I end up butchering it instead."

Lewis clamped the wine opener around the bottle, his eyes fixed on Calla. How did she know Carrie had always butchered the bread? Calla's familiar conversation and intimate knowledge frightened him.

As Calla cooked, Lewis sat on the bar stool, wondering if he should sneak out the front door. Whoever Calla was, she knew too much about his relationship with Carrie, to the point where only Lewis could tell Calla and Carrie apart. If he wasn't positive that he had buried Carrie a month ago …

"It's so stuffy in here. We must do something about the air conditioning now that it's summer, don't you think, Lewy? Why don't we eat on the balcony instead? Can you set it up while I finish cooking?"

Lewis nodded, unable to produce words, and grabbed plates and utensils. He pushed the slider open and stepped onto the balcony. The fresh air helped calm his nerves. He closed his eyes and let the air hit his face. *This is all a dream.*

"Lewy! Can you help me carry the shells? The pan is so heavy."

Lewis entered the kitchen and stared at the woman trying to impersonate Carrie and reminded himself that Calla and Carrie had different features. Carrie had high cheekbones. Calla's were sunken. Carrie had blue eyes; Calla had green. Lewis stared at Calla as he reached for the pan.

"Why, whatever is wrong, Lewy? Did you have a hard day at work? I'll give you a massage after dinner."

"Your eyes."

"Yes? Aren't they the prettiest shade of blue you've ever seen? You always tell me that, Lewy. It's enough to make a girl blush! Now get to the balcony before the shells turn cold."

She has blue eyes? At lunch yesterday, he remembered noticing Calla's green eyes. Green eyes and brown hair. Right? Lewis set the pan on the small table and eased himself into the chair. Who was the crazy one, him or Calla?

He pushed his chair to the far end of the balcony as Calla entered.

She placed a tray of garlic bread next to the shells and sat in the opposite chair.

Lewis scrutinized her face, trying to discover who was sharing his dinner.

"Should I make you a plate, Lewy?"

"Calla, I—" As she handed him the plate of shells, everything turned black.

LEWIS STRETCHED AND YAWNED. He rubbed his eyes and surveyed his bedroom. Calla, the dinner, her strange behavior—it had all been a dream. A long, dark, disturbing dream. Relieved, Lewis sat upright and smiled at the picture of Carrie on his nightstand. He caressed the frame. "How I miss you, babe." He kissed it and returned it to the nightstand.

"Why kiss my picture when you have the real thing?"

Lewis's eyes bulged. "Calla?"

"Who's Calla? Are you cheating on me?"

"Who are you?"

She strolled toward the bed and fixed her gaze on his. "I'm Carrie. Your *girlfriend?*"

Lewis backed toward the window as a blue light

emanated from her eyes. "Carrie died a month ago. I buried her."

"Did you? Are you sure, Lewis, I'm the one who died?"

"What do you mean? Of course, *she* died. I was there."

"You were there? What happened that night? Think, Lewy. Why did I die?"

Lewis covered his face with his hands. The night Carrie had died flashed across his mind. Carrie had been in the driver's seat, and a drunk driver had hit her head on. That's the memory he had, wasn't it?

"Remember, Lewy. Think about what happened. You were there, weren't you? You were at the accident."

Lewis squeezed his hands over his ears. *No. Make it stop. Go away.* The memories flooded back. The lights, the sirens, Carrie's blood over the dash. But she wasn't in the driver's seat, was she?

Lewis gulped as the figure moved closer, changing form until a blue demon-like creature stood before him. He couldn't escape his memories or this creature approaching him. He tripped over a chair and landed on the window seat, his body trembling as the enormity of his deeds washed over him.

"We know the truth, Lewis. We know what happened. And now it's your turn."

As the figure moved closer, Lewis leaned onto window and pushed it open. This was a dream too, wasn't it? He closed his eyes as he fell to the ground.

The demon, Carrie, and Calla surrounded him as he struggled to breathe. "We knew all along. Revenge is sweet, Lewy."

Love at the Pumpkin Patch

Marie McGrath

No *matches.* Brie Annenberg stared at the computer screen and resisted the urge to throw it out the window. How was it possible that on four dating websites she still had no matches? Wasn't it the point of these stupid algorithms to find her matches?

Brie growled at the screen.

"I know Halloween is in a few days, but must you really practice your growls? Are you expecting to scare the trick-or-treaters this year?" Alexis asked.

Brie closed her eyes. "Lex, go away."

"What's got your panties in a twist?"

Brie shoved the screen toward her sister. "This. This is my problem. The damn website is screwed. I have no matches! None."

Alexis rolled her eyes. "Well, go to a different site. It's not a big deal, Brie."

"This is the fourth website I've tried *today*!"

Alexis erupted in giggles.

"It's not funny."

"It kind of is."

Brie slumped in her chair. "What can I do? I'll be destined to be alone with my butterfly collection and hummingbird infatuation to keep me company."

"Why don't I set you up with someone?"

Brie scrunched her nose. "No, thanks. A blind date from you? Near Halloween?"

Alexis plopped on Brie's bed. "It could be fun, and besides, it doesn't appear you have many options."

Brie climbed over Alexis and grabbed a pillow. She launched it at her sister's head. "You suck."

Alexis shrugged. "You up for the date or not?"

Brie sighed. "I guess I don't have a choice."

"That's the spirit."

Brie watched as Alexis sauntered down the hallway. Was she really about to resort to a blind date that her sister set up? This couldn't be happening to her. She had been popular in high school and college. What had happened?

She glared at the computer screen and closed her laptop. She was desperate to not be alone, but she must be crazy to accept her sister's offer. Alexis wasn't known for having stable male friends. What kind of date would this turn out to be? Only time would tell.

"LEXI!" Brie shouted from her room.

It had been two days, and Alexis had ignored every question, every nudge about the blind date. She wouldn't crack, and it drove Brie nuts. Alexis wouldn't declare the date's name, age, occupation—nothing. Did he have a receding hairline? Was he tall? Short? Skinny?

"Calm down. You don't need to keep screaming."

"Well, it apparently is the only way I can get your attention. I'm dying. I need to know *something*."

Alexis shook her head. "Actually, you don't. He'll meet you at the pumpkin patch at five o'clock. So you better get dressed. It's almost time."

Brie's yellow and white polka dot sundress fluttered in the wind and fell mid-thigh as she surveyed her brown wedged sandals and fondled a small silver clutch purse. "I am dressed."

Alexis's eyebrows rose. "Oh."

Brie twirled around. "What? Why, *oh*? Do I need to change?"

"No, you're fine."

Brie crossed her arms. "Fine? I don't want to look *fine*. I want to be attractive and appealing. What if this is my last chance at happiness?"

Alexis rolled her eyes. "Don't be so dramatic, Brie. It isn't your last chance, and you look fine. Just not what I would wear."

Brie's eyebrows knitted. "Well, we can't all wear size zero tight black dresses. Besides, I'm going to a pumpkin patch, not a club."

"Remember who got you this date. You would do well to be grateful."

"I am." She sighed. "You started it."

Brie checked the time on her phone, shoved it back in her clutch and hugged her sister. It was time to go. "I hope you picked someone I'll like."

"I think you'll be satisfied with my choice."

Brie waved, grabbed her keys and went to her red Fiat. The drive to the pumpkin patch wouldn't be long. It was only a few miles from the house she shared with her sister. The closer to her arrival, the more her stomach knotted.

Meeting a complete stranger unnerved her. She didn't know his name or anything about what he would look like. She wasn't a vain person, but his physique would matter a little. She had to be attracted to him in some way. There were certainly dealbreakers, and she wasn't sure if her sister truly wanted to help or torture her slowly.

Brie pulled into the pumpkin patch's parking lot and surveyed the area crowded with several families. Pumpkins were as far and as wide as she could see. Alexis didn't say what they would do. Did he expect to pick a pumpkin and carve it? Or go on the hayride? Or the corn maze?

She shook her head. *Relax, Brie. Go with the flow.*

Brie gripped the clutch tightly and scanned the new arrivals. So far, no one was alone. Would she be stood up? That would be more embarrassing than going on a date with a loser.

She reached for her car door. Humiliation was not on the schedule. She would flee while she could.

"Brie?" a voice asked from behind.

Crap.

She was too late. She turned slowly to face the voice. "Yes?"

The voice had come from a tall man. He was delicious to look at. His brown hair was cut short, faded as it got closer to his neck and was thicker at the top. His eyes were a golden brown, and his smile was perfect.

He outstretched his hand. "My name is August Euler. I think I'm your date."

She shook his hand and felt the strong grip. His fingers were long and smooth. "It's nice to meet you, August." She diverted her gaze. "But I have to ask. How do you know my sister?"

He ran a hand through his hair. "I, ah, met her at the gym."

Brie's eyes rounded. "The gym?" She drew a breath. "Please tell me you didn't sleep with her before."

He gasped. "Absolutely not."

She breathed a sigh of relief. "Thank god. Sorry, it's Lexi, so I had to ask."

He chuckled. "I'll try to forgive the accusation." He proffered his hand and smiled. "Shall we head in?"

She nodded and looped her arm in his. She stared at him as long as she could. He was tall and tan. His legs were muscular under his brown khaki shorts, and his arms rippled under his polo. He had broad shoulders, and as far as Brie could tell was a drop-dead gorgeous specimen of a man. So why was he here with her and not married by now? Something had to be wrong with him. No man as gorgeous as that could be decent as well and still be available.

"So, what's your occupation?" Brie asked.

August handed money to the teller and grabbed their tickets. "I'm a lawyer."

Well, it wasn't his occupation that kept him single then.

"What about you?" he asked.

They walked through the gate arm in arm. "I'm a first-grade teacher."

"Ah, you love children."

Was this his flaw? "Yes. I do. You?"

He smiled wide. "Oh yeah. I'm the oldest of five. I helped my mom raise them."

"Yeah? That's so wonderful. Not many people would help their parents with their siblings."

He shrugged. "It was just us. My dad died when I was younger and my mom shouldn't do it all alone."

She nodded. Brie's family was intact, and, as far as her childhood went, she never prematurely had to be a caretaker. She was free to be a child; even now, if she wanted to, her parents would help her with bills. Her childhood was completely different from August's.

"Weird hobby?"

"Collecting buttons," he said.

"Hmm. Buttons? Any kind or …?"

"Yep. Anything goes. Small, large, wide, thin. All colors, materials, designs."

Brie scrunched her nose. "Why buttons?"

"I'm not really sure. My mom used to always hoard them. I suppose when you have that many children and you're a single parent, you learn to keep materials that could become useful later on. I would help her look at thrift stores and hobby shops. The crazier the better and I just continued doing it."

She smiled. "That's sweet. Not strange at all when you look at it that way."

"What about you?"

She rested her hand on her chin and contemplated. Did she choose something genuinely weird or something that could be loveable? "I collect recyclables."

"Recyclables? Like milk-carton type things?"

She nodded. "Yep."

"Projects for kids, right?"

Brie gasped. "How did you know?"

"Remember, lots of siblings and resourcefulness. It comes in handy."

She laughed. "That's very true. Most people think I'm crazy for keeping that stuff. They see it as junk, but I find so many ways to repurpose them."

"That's great, and it helps the environment too."

"Exactly."

Brie stole sideways glances. She had to admit this blind date was going much better than normal. Alexis was terrible with choosing men, and Brie had figured this would be no different. She was happy to be pleasantly surprised for once.

They approached a wagon filled to the brim with hay.

"Want to take a hayride?"

She nodded.

He proffered his hand and helped her onto the wagon.

She tucked her legs underneath and waited for him to sit. She beamed. "I love these things."

"So do I. Nothing says fall like a hayride."

She nodded. How were things going so well? She had expected to have a dud, but August was special. She could see herself with him, exploring their life. Could he be the one she was meant to find?

The wagon nearly burst with people before it moved. At the lurch of the wagon, August fell forward enough to brush her leg.

Her eyes gazed into his, and she smiled—then blushed.

"I'm sorry," he said.

She looked down. "No problem."

Brie surveyed the area. The hills were full of autumn decorations. Scarecrows and carefully placed pumpkins with wild corn adorned every corner.

"I hope you don't think I'm being forward."

The bridge of Brie's nose scrunched in response. "What do you mean?"

"How is a special woman like yourself still single? Am I missing something?"

Brie giggled. "I was wondering the same thing about you!"

He laughed. "Great minds."

"I'm not sure why I'm single. I guess I just hadn't found the right one yet."

"Hadn't?" He leaned closer. "Does that mean you have now?"

She shrugged. "Maybe."

A slow, sexy smile crept across his face. "I can work

with maybe." He scooted closer to Brie and rested his arm behind her as support. "What's your go-to snack?"

"Almonds. You?"

"Fruit snacks."

Brie's eyebrow rose. "Really?"

He chuckled. "Guilty."

"I didn't think anyone but my six-year-olds still ate those."

"Can't help it. Those things are addicting."

"I'll let my students know."

"Perfect Sunday?"

"Hmm. Sitting on my deck with a book and coffee."

"That sounds nice."

"It's my favorite. I look across the backyard and whisk myself away in a book of new lands and adventures. What about you?"

"Barbeque and bonfires with people I care about."

"That's pretty great too."

He readjusted his position and smiled. "Soda or tea?"

"Water."

"Interesting. I'm the same way."

"Really? No one usually agrees with that. I always get disgusted expressions and explanations that only when forced is water first. Or they have to add flavors."

"Really. Natural water, the perfect way to live."

August had to be too good to be true. Brie didn't know what to think. No one had ever aligned so easily in her life —let alone someone her sister had set her up with.

The wagon stopped, and Brie sighed. She was enjoying her time with August. The wagon ride soothed her nerves, and it allowed them to get to know each other. What else could they do? She didn't want the date to end yet.

August shielded his eyes from the setting sun. The glare angled perfectly to blind him.

Brie grabbed her sunglasses from inside her clutch. The sun intensified on its descent, not to mention she could use the sunglasses to hide her feelings behind the shield. If August figured out how she felt, would he run?

"It looks like a corn maze is over there. Wanna try?"

A corn maze? Those things always gave her the creeps. Brie shivered. "I don't know. I don't have the best sense of direction."

It wasn't a total lie, but it wasn't the main reason she didn't want to go.

August nudged her shoulder. "Come on. It'll be fun."

Brie stared at the jack-o'-lantern scarecrow guarding the entrance. Its hay poked through the middle of the shirt where its stomach would be. The pumpkin face carving looked deranged—haunted even.

She gulped and pushed down her instinct. Everything in her body said she didn't want to do this, but she was with August. What could go wrong? It was a harmless pumpkin patch; how much danger could she really be in?

THE THIRD DEAD end set Brie's nerves on fire. They were lost. They had to be lost. They were deep in the maze at this point. She could faintly hear the sounds from the rest of the pumpkin patch. How did someone *actually* get lost in a corn maze? Sure, it was in movies, but in real life? No.

"Are you sure it's this way?" Brie asked.

"Yeah, I think so. Look at the ground, no footprints, so we haven't been this way before."

"I guess."

August was great, but he didn't know how to navigate a corn maze, and all Brie wanted was to get out.

They turned the corner, and she slammed into the back of him.

"Ow," she said as she rubbed her nose. "Why'd you stop?"

He stayed silent and stared.

She peered around him, and on the dirt floor was a finger, cut from its body and bloody, in the middle of the path.

Brie screamed. "What the hell is *that*? I hope to god it's a prop." She nudged August forward and whispered, "Please be a prop."

August picked off part of the corn and swished it at the finger.

Brie gagged. "Definitely not a prop. Oh my god. How did someone lose that in here?"

August shrugged, still unable to find his voice.

A shrill scream echoed in Brie's ears. "What was that?" She ducked behind August and shivered. "What is happening? August, are you broken?"

He shook his head and cleared his throat. "I ... uh ... I'm sorry. I'm back. I just didn't expect to see a dead finger in the middle of a corn maze."

"You *think*?"

"We have to get out of here. Fast."

Well, no duh! What had he been trying to do this whole time? Get us lost?

"How do you propose we do that?"

"There's got to be a trick we can use." August looked around. "I've got it. I'll lift you above the corn, and you tell me which way we have to go."

"I'm going to do *what*? Are you crazy?"

"No. It'll work. Then we can get out before we figure out who that finger belonged to."

Brie gulped. "I suppose."

August kneeled while Brie shimmied up his back and onto his shoulders. He stood, and her head barely floated above the top of the corn maze. "I think we have to go left."

"You think?"

"Well, it's a little hard, since we seriously look like we're in the middle of nowhere."

"Left it is." August shifted his weight which caused Brie to scoot up a little higher.

"Oh my god. Put me down! Put me down!"

August quickly set her down. "What happened?"

"Shh!" Brie stood as still and as quiet as she could.

The corn rustled not far from where they waited.

"What is it?" August whispered.

Brie shoved her finger to her lips. *Maybe if we don't breathe, we will be safe.*

A man peered out of the corn carrying a dagger dripping with blood and wearing a pumpkin mask.

Brie backed up behind August and cowered.

August outstretched his hands in defense. "Hey man, we don't mean any harm. We just want out of the maze. Let us go, and we won't say anything, okay?"

The man growled like a feral cat.

Brie squeezed August's hand and whispered, "What should we do? He's clearly delusional."

August patted her arm. "I've got this."

The man stood inches from August.

"Sir? Can we talk about this? Let the pretty girl go, and we can work something out. Do you need money?"

The man cackled. "I don't want your money. I want *her.*"

"Her? Why her?"

Brie whimpered.

"No one leaves the maze, and you've brought me the prettiest *virgin* yet."

August's eyes bulged, and he whipped around to Brie.

How had the man known that? Brie never told anyone, *ever*. Not even Alexis knew she was still a virgin.

"Well, our mistake for entering your maze, but she hasn't done anything. Let her go."

Great, another way my inadequacy would ruin my life.

"Didn't you hear me, boy? No one leaves this maze. And she's *mine*."

August turned to face Brie and mouthed, *Run!* August shoved the man hard, but the man rebounded and stabbed August over and over in the stomach.

Brie gagged and lurched away from them both. She scampered through the paths as fast as she could, not knowing which way was the real way out. She came to a fork in the path and couldn't choose.

The sound of something dragging across the ground echoed in her ears. The man approached; she had to choose.

She ran left and kept going. The noise grew louder; she could hear the pumpkin patch once more. She would make it. She would get out.

After three more turns, Brie faced the outside. She exhaled and cheered. She had to leave; she wouldn't be safe until she was in her car and driving away. She stepped over the threshold of the maze, but something tugged at her foot. She turned to see the corn had wrapped around her ankles. She whipped herself back around.

No, no, no. She had made it this far; she couldn't get stuck now.

"Help!" she screamed.

The corn slowly closed in front of her, cutting her off to the rest of the undisturbed pumpkin patch. Something trickled down her arm. It was red. *Blood.* But where did it come from?

Brie noticed the man standing to her right in the corn, dripping the blood from his dagger down her arm.

It had to be August's blood. Who knew going into a corn maze would cause all this? And what's worse is she got him killed. This man didn't want anyone else but her. He hadn't deserved that fate.

Brie gagged and tried to scream, but the bile continued to rise in her throat. This was the worst date she had ever had.

The man scooted close to her and whispered into her hair, "I told you no one leaves the corn maze. *Stupid* girl. You'll pay for running."

Brie wept. "Please, just let me go."

The man laughed and yanked her down by her ankles.

She tried to fight him off, but she had nothing left. The corn had kept her from leaving; what kind of strength did she have to protect herself from that?

She laid helpless as the man dragged her around the corn maze and back to August. Her hair was full of dirt; her arms burned from the dirt floor.

The man dropped her next to August's body. He was pale and drained. Brie avoided looking at him. If she caught a glimpse of his face, she may never focus again. This was too much.

The man twisted the dagger in his hand. "What shall we do with you first?"

Brie swiped at her eyes. "Just kill me, if that's what your game is."

"Kill you? Why would I kill you when I can play with you as my pet forever?"

Brie wailed. "*Forever?* But won't others see?"

"Stupid girl. People see what they want to see."

"Are you saying I *wanted* to see you? To see that dead finger sliced off someone's body?"

"That's exactly what I'm saying."

"Why would I want to see that?"

"Because you wanted to be punished."

"Punished?"

How did this man know so deeply into her soul? How did he know she was a virgin, when the people closest to her never knew?

"You don't feel you deserve a man. You aren't worthy." He gestured around them. "So this is what you asked for."

"That's absurd. Regardless of wondering if I should have a guy like August, it doesn't mean I deserve this forever with you. Other people think things all the time, but this doesn't happen to them."

"Well, it does if they enter the maze and are virgins."

Calm down, Brie. This man is a lunatic. He's just trying to rile you up.

How had he made the corn move? Or grab her ankles? *Think, Brie!* How was this possible?

The man leapt toward Brie and snatched a handful of hair. "Don't worry. We'll have lots of fun together."

Brie spat in his face and grabbed the dagger. "The *hell* we will." She sliced her throat as fast as she could. The sensation was unlike anything she had ever felt. The blood pooled around her.

"*No!*" the man shouted.

Brie could feel herself slipping away. She didn't want to die, but she refused to play into whatever sick, twisted fate this was. This was her body, and she decided what happened to it. Her body felt heavy and weighted ... until it didn't. She floated above, staring at what she had left behind.

Her body laid next to August's, lifeless and covered in blood.

The man shouted at the air and pumped his fists. He removed his mask and threw it to the side. Long billowing hair spilled over his shoulders.

Brie hovered closer.

It wasn't a man at all. It was Alexis.

Alexis reached down and grabbed her sister. She screamed and called for someone.

August came from out of the corn maze and shouted.

What had happened?

If August walked out, who laid next to her body?

"Brie … no, no, no. I didn't mean for this to happen. You weren't supposed to give in. What did you do?"

"Lexi, oh my god! What the *hell*! You didn't say anything about this in the prank."

A prank? Her life had been wasted for a prank? Her sister wasn't always the nicest, but she didn't think she was cruel. Until now.

Alexis dropped Brie's body and shoved him. "She wasn't supposed to do that. It wasn't supposed to end like this." Alexis dropped to her knees and sobbed. "Brie, I'm so sorry."

Brie got close to her sister's ear and whispered, "You *killed* me, and now you have to live with it. I'll always be here, watching you. Don't slip up, or I'll know."

Alexis shivered as her eyes widened. Alexis didn't say anything to August, but Brie knew her message came across loud and clear.

How could her own sister play such a trick on her? She had taken her own life to avoid being taken in such a way.

She watched as Alexis continued to hold and cradle her body. She would never let her sister rest. For as long as she was alive, Brie would *never* rest again.

The Devil in the Details

Lo Potter

T he grey morning fell into a euphonic melody: cars, drizzling rain, and rumbles of thunder in the distance— a reprieve from the night's cacophony of violent storms. As the downtown streetlights dimmed for the coming day in the railroad town, The Daily Espresso came to life with its usual patrons bustling through its swinging wooden framed doors to the sound of a tinkling bell as a neon 'OPEN' sign lit up.

"Crazy weather we've been having. It's like the devil sent it." The old man chuckled and shook his head as he finished ringing up the customer and passed her a coffee. "Did you see the damage from the wind to the south of town?"

"Oh, yes." The sterling haired woman nodded, lifting her cup to her lips. "Carl got called out in the middle of the night to clear three trees from the highway." She paused, surveying the cafe for new faces, passing over a man hidden behind a newspaper by the window. She leaned in, whispering, "Did you hear about Miss Wilson?" She picked up her scone from the counter.

"I'm 'fraid so. My police scanner caught it early this morning." He solemnly nodded, adding, "It woke me up. Has anyone heard anything yet?" The old man leaned closer, joining the woman in her perusing of the sparsely populated room, except the regulars and one new face by the front window reading a morning newspaper and drinking regular black coffee.

"What happened to Hannah Wilson, Harry?" An eavesdropping young woman with a bottled red pixie cut and a plastic-wrapped muffin came up behind their conversation and the plated scone. As Harry made eye contact, she added, "I'll have a large mug latte with a pump of that hazelnut and chocolate syrup."

"You kids and your damn sugar. That ain't coffee." The three smiled in a static levity before Harry looked out across his cafe at nothing in particular. He frowned. "They say she's missin'."

"Missing? She's not that much older than me. Why, wasn't she prom queen or something?" She chewed her lip, eating off her lipstick.

"Now, Winnie, she was a debutante for sure, but I don't know about a prom queen." The older woman's cheeks rounded as she smiled condescendingly at the younger woman.

"Anything missing from the home?" Winnie pressed, paying no mind and nudging the sterling haired biddy out of the way.

"Nothing's missing except her, according to the scanner," Harry responded, getting back to brewing Winnie's strange beverage in between his batches of fresh single-origin roast and stocking the bakery display with the morning's fresh deliveries. "Dispatch got a call from a neighbor after she didn't respond. They tried to see if she was okay when they noticed the hole in her roof from the storm."

"Well, that's distressing," Winnie frowned and looked towards the older woman as she nodded to indicate that she had decided on a table. Winnie put a few dollars on the counter for her coffee and muffin, then sat at a table with her elder. "Did you know her well, Mrs. Ada?"

"I taught Miss Wilson piano lessons when she was a little girl. She was always a troublemaker; didn't want to practice, always looking for an easy way out. Who knows what she got herself into this time?" Mrs. Ada grunted, popping a chunk of scone into her mouth, followed by a swig of coffee. As she chewed, her jaw rocked side to side like a metronome with loose denture fixative.

A young man from a nearby table with circles under his eyes leaned over. "I was there last night. I did the write up for the paper." He reached out towards Winnie for an introduction. "I'm Ben Jones, crime beat reporter for the Independent." Though sparse with facial hair, the young man's charisma made friends for him.

Winnie's eyes locked on his bare left ring finger as she shook his hand and examined his features. As she flirted with his eyes, her lips twitched into a smile. "Winifred Simmons, but everyone calls me Winnie." Half his grin increased in height on his face. She brushed her bangs back with her hand and asked with earnest, "What did you see?" Her eyes widened, and her pupils dilated.

The man in the corner by the window adjusted his shirt collar and newspaper, surveying the room. While Ben and Winnie heard the crinkle of the pages, neither turned their heads. "The house was covered in blood," Ben confessed under his breath to Winnie. "I think she was murdered." He leaned over and rested his hand on the women's cafe table next to Winnie's resting palm.

"Murdered?" Mrs. Ada exclaimed, only to be hushed by several voices in the room.

"Why else would there have been so much blood? Did she like to slaughter her old chickens?" the reporter half-joked toward Winnie, tilting his head and flattening his mouth.

"Miss Wilson grew up the daughter of the former mayor. She wouldn't know which end of the chicken to cut off to get it to stop clucking." Mrs. Ada deadpanned at the young man. "What in the world did she get herself involved in? Was anything missing?"

The man in the corner watched them over the top of his newspaper, thumbing his black felt hat's brim on his table. Over the back of his chair, a tan jacket dripped into the puddle of water on the floor beneath it. Dropping his hat's brim, he lifted his cup of coffee to his lips and slurped the black brew. He smiled as not a single patron turned their heads toward him.

Ben looked back and forth between the two women. "The sheriff wouldn't say much, but I snooped around the mayor's mansion a bit once they would let me go in with the crime scene photographer." He looked up at the ceiling in thought for a moment, then continued, "I think she got mixed up with someone or something. Young and beautiful woman, naïve to the ways of the world. She falls in love and is taken advantage of. Happens all the time." He gesticulated as he told his wild theory. "The house had been ransacked. There was a fight. She struggled." He shrugged, adding, "And that's the story I'm writing." Ben took a long drink of his coffee.

"I don't think that's the case at all," Mrs. Ada declared as Ben choked. "I bet she pissed someone off. They couldn't take it anymore and snapped. She always left a wake of destruction behind her, even as a child. She pushed her luck with me constantly. As her piano teacher, I promise she was a right pain in my ass." She leaned in, her eyes shifting between Winnie and Ben as he switched to a chair at their table. Mrs. Ada whispered to the two young adults, "I prayed for that child. Save her soul, you should have seen what she did to her poor mother's rose bushes. It must have taken an act of God for them to survive. I can't imagine what being in a relationship with her must have been like." She shook her head, staring at her lap. She then lifted her face and turned to Ben and Winnie. "Was she seeing anyone?"

The reporter delayed, changing mental gears. "One of the security cameras caught a man in a long coat and a pork pie hat going into the house last night."

The man in the corner near the window lowered his newspaper half an inch below his eye level while angled toward the three. Rain pelted the windows, and the lights inside the cafe flickered in response to another clap of thunder.

Harry wiped his hands on a rag at the counter before walking towards the group. He turned a chair around from Ben's prior table and straddled it, joining them. "Try to keep your voices down," he insisted, before joining in. "Do you really think she's dead? My daughter knew her all through school. They did choir together and were once peas in a pod, you'd say."

"If she isn't, someone is. There was a lot of blood." The reporter's frown sank further as it transformed into a largemouth bass impersonation. The group sat in silence while Harry did a round of coffee refills for the room. Upon his return, Ben asked, "What did your daughter think of Miss Wilson?"

"In high school, she spouted off all kinds of things, and it ruined their friendship. Started rumors that the mayor was into devil worship and that kind of nonsense," Harry said, setting down the carafe and rejoining the group.

"What kind of rumors?" Ben rotated and tilted his head five degrees toward Harry at full attention. Under the table, he slipped a notepad and golf pencil from his pocket, jotting notes on his knee.

"Daddy, stop it!" A young woman with humid ringlets pulled back into a ponytail stormed over. She wore a black t-shirt, jeans, and an apron and swore under her breath as she marched over with a bus tray. "I hate it when you talk about me. What's this about?"

"I'm a reporter from the Independent." Ben paused and looked at the young woman as she grabbed the empty scone plate, ignoring him with a scowl. "We're talking about the disappearance of Miss Hannah Wilson last night."

The plate shattered when it hit the floor. "Hannah is missing?"

"Yes, Jenny. That's why this nice young man—what's your name?" Harry turned his attention to Ben.

"Ben Jones, sir."

"That's why Ben here is asking questions about what might have happened. It made me think about how you and her used to be so close." Harry stood and put a hand on his daughter's shoulder as he trudged to get a broom and dustpan for the remains of the plate.

She stood there in silence for a few breaths with her eyes closed, then she opened them and looked at Ben. "Did you find anything at the house?" Jenny narrowed her green eyes, her jaw clenched.

"Nothing was taken," Ben reassured her, confused.

"But there was that big stink you made senior year of high school," Harry continued as he rejoined the group and began sweeping the debris, "saying that the whole family was involved in devil worship and occult stuff." Harry tightened his face, his mouth slanted and eyebrows knotted as he dumped the dustpan and returned to the group, grasping Jenny's shoulder. "My daughter stopped wanting to be friends after something happened. She said Hannah's family made deals with the devil. Claimed Hannah wanted to tattoo some protection symbol on her when they were teens. Wanting to force my daughter into a tattoo was enough for me. You tell the story, hun."

Jenny crossed her arms and looked away. "I really should be getting back to work, Dad."

The reporter's eyes went wide. "Now that you mention it, I did see some strange stuff in the house." He hesitated; hand raised in consideration of grasping his chin. "Strange symbols under rugs and behind paintings— smeared by rainwater that leaked through the roof that night after a large branch fell on the place."

Jenny closed her eyes. "The Wilsons were the town morticians up until Hannah's daddy closed the funeral parlor to run for Mayor. The story she told me went that the blood from embalming the bodies was the secret to his grandmother and mother's success with their prize-winning rose bushes." She opened her eyes.

Ben's notepad sat open on the table as he hung on her every word. Winnie's mouth hung agape. Mrs. Ada swallowed.

Jenny continued, "Every year, her parents had this big party right before the state fair. Hannah joked that it was the kind of party everyone was just dying to see." Her voice vibrated in between laughter and trembling. "That last year she said I could come, but only if I tattooed this weird looking thing on me for protection. That way, I couldn't be chosen." Jenny looked to her right periphery and crossed her arms, rubbing them. She then looked to her left, catching a glimpse of a newspaper being shuffled. She lowered her volume, adding, "Some of the mayor's employees had that tattoo."

Mrs. Ada rolled her eyes and huffed. "That story is complete nonsense! Her mother died last year, and her father the year before that! The year before her father's death was the last party that house saw and Hannah graduated from high school." The old woman pursed her lips and dabbed crumbs from her face. "Sounds like childish make believe."

Jenny shrugged at her and walked off with Harry's carafe. "You know she was a demon child."

The three patrons and Harry all looked at each other before Harry stood up to get back to the counter. "So, where's the body if she's dead? Did you see drag marks?"

Mrs. Ada's eyes widened, and her face tightened with the corners turned down. "Harry! That's highly inappropriate."

"She could have been carried," Ben interrupted. "The description says she wasn't a very big woman."

Winnie scrolled through her phone looking at pictures of Hannah. "She always looked so beautiful without even trying. We'd all been certain she was going to become a famous Instagram model or something. Get out of this place. Maybe she's gone."

She flicked her finger a few more times until she came upon a picture of Hannah with her picture-perfect smile next to her family's prize-winning roses from the state fair with the caption, 'I'm so lucky to be the fourth generation of Wilson women to win this award #nofilter #blessed. Remember Rainstorms Bring Roses!'

The man in the corner removed his hat from the tabletop and placed it on his head, standing to put on his tan trench coat and securing the belt at the waist. As he turned to the room, he locked eyes with Ben. Winnie flinched as an invisible force ran an electric chill up her spine. Ben watched as the man strode up behind Winnie's chair, adjusting his black pork pie hat. Though she never turned around, his mouth moved, and Winnie trembled with recognition. The man spread a sinister smile of perfect white teeth, each like a headstone, towards Ben. Winnie's chest began rising and falling faster as her eyes widened, her entire body stiff as the man drew closer, leaning over her.

The man turned around and sauntered out of the cafe as Ben grabbed Winnie's hand, shaking her. "What did he say? Winnie? Are you okay?" Ben hesitated as Winnie failed to respond, her eyes fixated on the air in front of her. "Winnie?"

Her face was drained of color. She took a deep inhale, gasping to break her shallow breathing pattern as she searched Ben's eyes and face. Mrs. Ada covered her mouth with her lace handkerchief as she watched the strange man in the tan jacket and wool hat stride from view through the window.

Winnie took one more deep breath and whispered, "He said," she paused, her voice wavering slightly, "'She looks beautiful under her rose bushes'." Tears ran down her cheeks. Shaking and standing, she rushed to the waste bin next to the register by the counter.

Running to Harry, Ben pressed him. "Harry, who was that customer in the tan trench coat and black hat? Have you seen him before?"

Winnie vomited into the trash can beside him, a cloud of flies emerging from the trash can buzzing around her head as she cried. Harry stared, shaking as Jenny ran over and pulled Winnie's head back, patting her shoulder and swatting away the flies. "Dad! Who was that man? Tell him!"

Harry's petrified face shifted as his mouth hung open, words unable to escape into the buzzing cloud of flies and clapping thunder.

Ben sprinted through the door into the maelstrom, the drops against the metal roof drowning out the sweet tinkling of the bell on the shop's door. "Come back here! I have a few questions!" He chased after the man as the raindrops grew larger and heavier, leaving red welts where each struck his skin and slowing his movements. Unable to see, he lifted his hand to his forehead attempting to shield his eyes. "Sir! Wait!"

He rushed after the man who continued to walk at a casual pace, always a few steps ahead. With a clap of lightning, the streets of their railroad town lit up white, then darkened beneath the green-black storm clouds. For a moment, the man vanished into the torrent gathering into the rushing waters consuming the street drains and sidewalks.

"Why are you following me, Ben?" a melodious, familiar voice inquired from behind–the vibrations cascading through his nervous system. The sound gripped his throat from the bottom of his gut.

When Ben spun around, he failed to find the source through the blinding, pelting raindrops and lightning. "Who are you?" He searched through the squall as each drop fell harder, visibly bruising his skin. "Did you kill Hannah Wilson?" he shouted into the maelstrom. The man raised a single hand as Ben neared and with an enigmatic smirk, he snapped.

And with that, the clouds vanished. Ben squinted upwards into pristine blue skies while the sun cast western leaning shadows of the hundred-year-old buildings across the grid pattern downtown. Shoving his hands into his pockets, a chill setting in through his sopping clothes as he spun on the squeaking heel of his saturated leather shoe. Checking behind the Bradford Pear trees and benches, no trace of the man in the tan trench coat remained, as if it were a figment of his imagination or an evaporating dream like the mists now rising from the empty streets.

Alone, he receded to the cafe with his head hung low. Placing his hand upon the door, he looked back over his shoulder at the street as a light breeze blew past him, generating a slight whistling whisper in his ear.

Devil's in the details, ain't it?

A Day at the Fair

Jinny Alexander

I hear ye's asking about the townsfolk round here? What ye want to know about them for ain't my business, but there ain't much I don't see from up here in this old lighthouse. Let me tell ye about that one down there, look—there now, ye see him down yonder? Benedict Carson. Used to be a fine enough man afore the tragedy. What happened to Benedict near about, destroyed him. He ain't been the same since that night. Used to be pals, so we did ... used to be in the same class way back when we was boys. Long time ago, that were. I remember one time, we was sitting in class and be done put a frog in wee Cora's bag, God rest her soul too—there's another story right there. Full of life and tricks we were back then. And then he met his wife, and they married and had the prettiest wee bairn and bought up a little cottage down there in the town, yonder. See that row down there? Second one in, they set up a right bonny little home ... Ye'd find him down at the church most days, beyond the town square, there, do ye see it?

...

ON THE CONSOLE in the sacristy, a walkie-talkie crackles a fragmented message. The robed figure swigs *Vin Santo* straight from a bottle and snatches the radio up off the surface. I can't hear what he mumbles into the mouthpiece; his back is to me, and the stained glass distorts my view. I rap gently on the glass, and he swings toward the sound, walkie-talkie in one hand, bottle in the other. I move to the door and push it with my foot.

In the moment between the window and the door, the cleric has rearranged his demeanor. The wine is stoppered; the walkie-talkie out of sight—stuffed in a drawer? Beneath his voluptuous robe? Tossed casually into that large golden chalice on the altar-like table behind him? Perhaps I'd imagined it. I must calm down. Breathe. Breathe.

"May I help you?" His dulcet tones tingle along the back of my neck like mice running along the keys of the church organ.

I'd looked in the church first; a somber, cold building filled with dark wood and heavy silence. Grey tombstones line the aisles; their heavy lids holding closed the resting places of the town's most revered, entombed within this sacred building. I'd beaten a hasty exit, the stillness oppressive as I stood amongst too many memories of the town's long-dead. The churchyard looked no more welcoming; I would look for signs of life before I further studied the dead. And here I am, face to face with the vicar … rector … whatever he calls himself. I detect a whiff of what may be incense but smells a lot like whiskey and tobacco. An old-fashioned typewriter nestles on a small desk, catching dust rays in a sun-beamed alcove.

I introduce myself, but not by name. I hold out my

hand and am met in return with a surprisingly strong grip. A liver-spotted, tanned, well-worn hand with dirt under the nails that is at odds with the cleanliness I'd expected from a churchman. I hear my mother's frustrated voice echoing in a childhood memory: *Cleanliness is next to Godliness, child. Would you ever scrub under those nails?*

"You're asking about the townsfolk." It isn't a question. The walkie-talkie, I think. He already knows why I'm here, so I nod.

"The lighthouse keeper said come here if I wanted to know about ..." I hesitate, searching for words. "The town history." I improvise a little, aiming for politeness. Again, he knows exactly what I haven't asked.

"Ben Carson." He nods towards the door. "He's the groundsman here. When he's able for it."

As I wander around the graveyard, the evening sun comes out again. Contrarily, the warmth and brightness make me shiver, as the graves are thrown into deep shadows painted black by the ancient yew trees along the wall. Under cloud, the cemetery had been colored in the mellow hues of a cobbled pathway, a worn brick wall, patched with moss and yellowing lichens. The sun, however, draws sharp edges and hard lines. As the sky brightens, the graveyard darkens. A man stoops over a tidy grave, a drooping bunch of something yellow wilting in his hand. He strokes the headstone, tender as a lover's touch, his grief raw as he bends his head to rest it on the stone. I turn away. In the shadow of a holly tree, a straggly, weather-beaten man leans on a shovel to support his shabby frame.

I know, even from this distance, that this propped-up figure is Ben Carson. The groundsman. I would know him from anywhere, despite the change.

Although he is the one I've come for, I'm not ready.

Not yet. I stay behind the shadow of tombstones, under shelter of a drooping yew branch. His face is directed towards the grieving man, but his eyes, I know, are vacant and his mind elsewhere. I can be sure of that. I remain hidden, watching, biding my time. The sorrowful widower leaves, reluctantly, looking back at the grave. The sinking sun bounces off the gold star badge on his chest, replicating a tiny flashlight beam sweeping uselessly across the path.

Ben lays down his shovel and follows from a distance, ducking unsteadily between crooked headstones.

When they are out of sight, I move to the grave the sheriff left. *Cora Harris.* I touch the cold stone and wish her peaceful repose. Her grave is still fresh, tended well; there has not yet been time for moss to settle or his grief to ease. A few years. I trace the date with my fingertip, but I don't need to trace her name to feel the curves and lines of her presence etched into the marble.

I murmur words to Cora I've said before. I doubt she hears them. My words are as futile as a searchlight on a stormy night. I don't linger here.

Where Ben had been standing is a patch of bright green. It's fenced with a low picket, the grass even and free of weeds. There's no mound; no body lies beneath. It's not a grave, yet flowers have been placed atop. They have been arranged with care, although their petals drift haphazardly onto the green. A prickle runs along my spine. I shudder in the dying sunlight as I turn and walk back towards the town, the store, the fairground. I remember these streets as if it were yesterday. As if I had not been away.

I follow Ben, at a distance. I don't want him to recognize me. Not yet. He ducks around the back of the library. I think he's stopping for a piss, but instead, he goes to a window and pries the frame. He clambers in—not as if it's the first time. He knows where to grab the frame, where to slide the tip of his boot into a crevasse, and how to twist his shoulders just so. It creaks around his slight body as he climbs through. Though he pulls the window shut behind him, when I creep closer, I see it doesn't close. The frame is twisted. His disturbance has caused the ancient wood to shed flakes of paint onto the crackled sill. I slide my back against the pebble-dashed back wall and feel waves of fatigue clamber up my body. Aching legs. A dull thump in my lower back. Heaviness pressing on my temples.

I let my eyes close. Rough paint prickles through the wool of my hat. The perfect silence of a closed library gives a moment of sanctuary in the storm of my day. I long to sleep, but it's too risky to stay here, so I force my eyelids open and push my hands to the ground beneath my thighs, levering my aching body semi-upright again. I won't stand fully erect. I need to stay below the window, out of sight.

I walk away, backwards, watching. A flickering light moves slowly beyond the windows. I make out the shadow of bookcases, but the light is low, shimmering like a paranormal specter. As I watch, darkness falls. I turn and walk away, on the south-easterly road towards the marshes, past the cinema's neon promise of a late-night horror show. I pull my coat tighter, duck my head further into my scarf, and push open the tavern door.

Above the bar, the name on the license matches the name on the pub's shoddy exterior: *Paddy Flannery, proprietor, Flannery's Tavern*, followed by a string of numbers that mean nothing or something. He doesn't glance twice as I murmur my order from behind my scarf. I've regained the weight, changed my hair, but I'll take no chances yet. My winter clothes offer easy disguise, and for that, I'm grateful.

I wave the glass loosely at the change he proffers, turning towards a dim corner. A fire belches more smoke than warmth, but I let the fug shroud me, happy to become mist while whiskey warms me and dulls the aches.

Paddy fumbles behind the bar, pretending to be busy, but he's been polishing one glass for the last ten minutes. He's as distracted as everyone in this stinking town, and I remember why I left as if it had been a choice I'd made. I push the memories back down to the bottom of my glass, swirling, swishing, swigging them back in a swallow I'm sure is audible to the room. The whiskey assaults my gut, scorching my insides, and I beckon Paddy for another with a raise of the empty glass.

Up in the lighthouse, Jeremiah hadn't seemed to know me. In the church, the vicar was new since I was here last, the church itself unfamiliar ground under my feet. Will my luck hold with Paddy? I keep my head down as he slides the fresh glass across the table on a slick of spilled dreams. I shouldn't stay, but the lure of drink and near-warmth is strong. I want to thaw before I face the marsh road; the battered boarding house; my paltry life packed into an old army knapsack stenciled in broken black ink with the address of the asylum.

I drank here with Ben before I left town, before he sank into the depths of his own amber solace. He used to be a happier man; the drinking came later, after *then* but before I went. By the time I couldn't face staying, and he couldn't leave, the only hopes he could find were those he could see through the distortions of a golden inch in a whiskey glass. It was only a short slide from the bottom of the first empty bottle to making damn sure he always kept his glass half full. It was sixteen months later I heard he'd lost the house. I'd divorced him long before then, of course. *Sleeps rough, he does*, the vicar had said earlier today, his eyes flickering towards the organ loft betraying it as one bedding place. I guess that the cozy calm of the library offers another if the flickering lights and broken window are anything to go by.

...

A BELL JANGLES DIMLY in the far reaches of the Curiosity Shop as I push the door open and leave the morning outside.

"My little Caramel Cupcake," the man murmurs from behind the counter, stretching out a gnarled hand as if to greet me but withholding it inches from my own. "You're back."

I should have known that my identity would not remain hidden from Herb Korver, a man who knows everything and misses nothing. A small shiver threatens to raise the hairs on my neck, then retreats as I relax for the first time since coming back. Here, at least, I can stop pretending. Here, I can ask for answers.

Yes, I think, *I'm back*. I don't think I've said it aloud, but he hears me anyway, grins his slow smile, and points a bony finger towards a display case to the left of the shop. As I turn to look, he pushes a walkie-talkie behind a stack of papers impaled on a tall, thin spike. The sight of the spike chills me more than the walkie-talkie; by now, I've become accustomed to the trail of airwaves announcing my passage around the town, but I don't think Herb Korver will spill my identity yet. He is a man of many secrets, but he collects rather than shares them. It seems strange to think that of all the townsfolk I would trust in this one—a man I had had little to do with and no reason to like. Still he was benevolent once, I recall.

I half turn, unwilling to put my back fully to Mr. Korver, and pull open the cabinet's glass door. It hangs a little loose on its hinges, a delicate key dangling partway out of the lock. Still half-watching Mr. Korver, I reach out for the first item that catches my eye: an exquisitely carved wooden jewelry box, also boasting a tiny keyhole and intricate key.

A slight movement from the proprietor stops my reach; his head shakes almost unperceptively, but a tiny change in the air transmits his message clearly: *not that*. My hand brushes against a crackled statuette. The little figurine is desolate, old fashioned china in a blue and white dress. Her right hand is missing, her coloring like my own. She looks bereft, unloved, and hopelessly lost. I stroke her porcelain dress with a gentle finger as I look beyond her to see what Mr. Korver was prompting me towards. Not her, anyway. I know who she is already: a sculpted depiction of a broken-hearted girl, as tiny and unreachable as the figure reflected in Ben's eyes when I'd first walked away. My right hand. Severed and useless, drowning in sorrow and drink. Not her. She will give me no answers.

"Further back," Herb Korver emits the words as a low growl, faint as a kitten's purr but with the strength of a lion.

This? I look back at him. No, he shakes his head, the smallest movement. *This?* No. Not that. We play this game for moments more until I rest a finger on a brass telescope. As I feel its smooth coolness, I know it is this that he has drawn me towards. My back is cold, despite the thickness of my coat. I glance towards him, and the slightest incline of his chin confirms that this is the object I sought.

He reaches for the walkie-talkie, as if to transmit to

someone, but retracts his hand before it touches the radio. "Who would care? Who is watching me?" He shrugs; the tiniest of movements as his shoulders lift in his jacket then fall again. "It's what you can see," he says, "and it's what has been seen. Take it. I am not an unkind man. Take it. Return it when you have your answers." He holds my gaze, making certain that I'm watching, before pushing the walkie-talkie further away. "In this shop, my Delectable Donut, I also sell time. I am not an unkind man, and you have suffered enough."

I leave the shop, twisting the telescope in my hands, playing with its reassuring solidness, its careful weight. I walk aimlessly, the brass spyglass warming at my touch. Salt stings my eyes. The familiar screeching of gulls rips my heart as I stumble over a rocky path. I wipe tears of wind and sea spray from my eyes and find I'm at the lighthouse door again. The door swings open before I reach it, and Jeremiah's dark face peers out into the daylight.

I push back my hood, looking up at his weatherworn face, challenging him to see me for who I am this time.

"Jeremiah." As I say his name, he backs heavily into an old captain's chair.

"I knowed it were ye," he says, "I knowed it were ye yesserday. What ye come back for? There ain't nowt can be done after all this time. Ye know, that don't ye?" He doesn't make it a question. "Did ye find Benedict, then?"

"I saw him," I say, "I saw him all right. He didn't see me. Not yet. How is he, Jer? How's he been?"

Jeremiah moves as a man far older than his years, busying himself away from me, gathering thoughts before he speaks. I find it hard to remember he's only the same age as Ben ... but we've all aged some in the last few years ... He bustles with the kettle, placing it down on the modern enamel stove that seems incongruous in these ancient round walls. The old sadness radiates from him as he puts both hands on the counter and sighs deeply. It's as I had guessed then. Ben has not recovered. Jer's silence answers me clearer than words.

"That bad, huh? I hear he's sleeping rough?"

"Aye, stops here many a night, he do. Likes to be up in the tower and look out over town. Thinks he'll see her if he looks hard enough. Watches for her through the lightroom window and his bottle. It blurs into what he finds in his mem'ries once he's downed enough. I reckon he'll fall headlong down them stairs." He gestures with a nod towards the spiral steps. "I reckon many a time he'd like to do jus' that. Put an end to it. Other times, he beds down in the church, the library, the old cabin up yonder mountain path, anywhere he winds up after the pub throws him out …"

Jeremiah breaks off and chuckles; a deep, throaty laugh that I remember from before. "There's some around here thinks places do be haunted, but mos' times it's jus' yer Benedict lookin' for a place to sleep it off. He tried to sober up a-while back, tried again after Sheriff Harris arrested him. He had to in the end, for his own good—but ain't no good. There's always more hope in a bottle than in sobriety …"

He tails off again, looking for happier times in the swirls the sugar spoon draws in his mug. I lay the little telescope on the table between us, looking up at Jeremiah.

"What's this, Jer? What's this got to do with it?"

Jeremiah stretches out his arm and gives the brass instrument a twist that sends it spinning around in lazy circles.

"I ain't seen this for a long while," he said, "Not since…" Abruptly he drops his hand down, stopping the telescope's spin and pinning it to the table. He looks straight at me, his black eyes locking firmly onto my own. "Not since yer wee one dis'peared that night. 'Twas on the table in the light room that night. And I ain't never seen it since." He lets go of it, scratches his ear. "Where'd ye get it from?"

Before I've even finished saying the name, he's reached for the walkie-talkie, bringing it to his lips and pressing the transmit button. I close my mouth and don't bother to finish. He mutters into it, numbers and jargon, and then "Who? Who'd ye get it from, Herb?" There's an inaudible crackle of reply. He clicks off the handset and looks at it as if it were still giving him answers. The air still holds the weight of static as something passes between us in the stare Jeremiah gives me.

"He dinna say much, but he said enough. 'Twas Ted Brunel—ne'er did trust him—knew there were sommat slippery 'bout him, always did say that about him e'er since I done caught him flashing boats up on the rocks back them years ago when I were just a young 'un. Ne'er knew he were back here that night ... not till after ... what with everyone out searchin'. There were too many townsfolk comin' and goin' to know who were where. Musta come back here after he told us all t' get out on them rocks an' search for your wee lass. He musta ..." Jeremiah gazes out over the Devil's Hand, and I do too. The silence between us fills with memories.

"Where've ye been, Lise?" Jeremiah eventually breaks the silence. I warm my hands around the mug and try to still my shivers. It's cozy in here with the stove, but the chill inside me never thaws. The care in his voice brings new tears, but I can't answer him. Not until I've talked to Ben. I owe him the answers first, I think. Jeremiah understands.

The radio crackles to life again, as he summons the man I was married to.

...

WORD SPREADS FAST ROUND HERE, and Ben comes as soon as he hears. I look into the red rimmed eyes I used to drown in, hoping for a glimpse of a life belt. All I see is my own reflection, minute and doubled—left and right—a tiny speck in his memory, a particle of a life lost. I barely hear his question, only for that I know what he is asking. *Why are you here? Why did you come back?*

I can't tell him. I can't tell him I never went away. That all this time I've been here in town, under the shadow of the lighthouse, locked away in Wilmington Asylum since they took me out of the hospital not long after I left him drowning in the bottom of a glass. I can't tell him yet that after I left him, there was nothing else to wait for. Not since our little girl disappeared. Not since that day at the fair when one minute she was there with us, swinging off our hands and asking for cotton candy and then, in a heartbeat, she was gone. I can't tell him now that after the first years of *hanging in there*, or *she'll turn up*, or *we'll find her* had begun to wear as thin as silk thread; that after the gossamer eventually, finally, snapped, that once he lost himself looking for her in the bottom of every bottle, that after I left him, I had nowhere to go but down.

I broke.

I woke with, bandaged wrists and bruises dark as plums under my eyes. With no next of kin holding vigil by my bedside, they locked me away in Wilmington. They made it sound like a choice—I could pull myself together, contact my family, let the doctors help me, but I turned my face to the wall and wished I had died, so they wheeled me off to the asylum. They locked me in a room with only the smallest skylight—*nothing to escape from, my dear, we'll keep you safe now*—for a glimpse of the days I tallied with a red crayon, strokes red and thick as blood on the wall above my bed. Only a thin mattress without sheets—*nothing to put around your neck my dear, for your own good*—and only spoons to eat with—*no knives, my dear.*

I woke to the sound of crows pecking on the roof. I fell asleep to owls crying in the forest beyond the walls. By day, gulls screeched above me, calling mournfully over the harbor. While I could no longer search for our daughter, they screamed her name across the water as if they alone may still find her.

Don't make me remember. Don't make me remember.

Beyond these dark walls, I hear the sun's rays hitting off cracked earth. Loud, too loud. The brightness stings my eyes. I rock backwards. I taste the bitter sharpness of metal as I bite down through the sunbeams that fall from the skylight. If I can only hold them, I will find her again. The remembrance of her conjures a breeze, wafting the glow of gorse through my mind. It dazzles and burns. The coconut scent of summer—that day we try to remember and try to forget.

The crows peck at the roof.

I rest my head against grey-green walls. Their padding is the dingy green overcooked cabbage of her childhood. I tried to feed us well, on our paltry budget that stretched to diapers and baby food but never as far as a good meal for the two of us too. Our daughter ate well; we made sure of that.

Shut out the color, close my eyes against that cabbage-grey … I shut out color, but smell pervades.

I crumple to the floor like discarded underwear awaiting launder.

The damp aroma of greying cabbage takes me home, home to us, a family of three. You, Benedict Carson, my handsome husband, my childhood love, my all; me, still a little overweight from carrying her, but gaunt around the eyes from sleepless nights and worry of feeding my family on our meagre earnings; her, the light of our life, our world, our reason. Small, she clings to my legs in the Formica kitchen. I tousle her head with weary hands, before resuming my efforts to put food on the table.

'It's the thought that counts,' you always said, kissing me gently on the forehead, scratchy from a day's stubble. We climbed out of it; that interlude of hardship … I went to work, we got by, our baby girl grew into knee socks, buckle shoes, school uniform, scabby knees … a day at the fair.

As I sit here with Ben at Jeremiah's table, my mind races, blurred with memories that whirl with all the color and brightness of a fair ride.

She is there, on the Waltzers, whirring, laughing; her head thrown back in joy. Her long braids are swinging, tied in green gingham ribbons. Now, dizzy, she runs towards the carousel. Horses dance and spin. My thoughts gallop onwards, blurring, creating a breeze that make the chains rattle, except—now, there are no chains—now, here in the asylum, my safety restraints are served up in tiny orange capsules and a padded room.

They are despatched as regularly as a crow pecking on the roof, by an orderly in a uniform.

He measures the dose with a smile as sweet as the candy floss of a stranger's lure as it intercepts a child on her way towards the carousel. Is that what happened? A stranger with a ball of puffy cotton candy as pink as a child? The frantic jolliness of the barrel organ plays the soundtrack in my mind. I taste sickly sweet candy floss, and bile rises in my throat …

The colors scream and swirl together, turning towards the inevitable black.

It's always the thoughts that count.

BEN SPEAKS. I don't hear what he says. He puts a tentative hand on my arm, pulling me out of my memories. He twists me towards him and tries to look in my eyes. His are unfocused, still heavy with last night's drink. I can tell as I look at his unkempt clothes, his straggle of beard, the dirt under his nails that he is the man I left and not the man I married. I want to ask him all the questions that half-form in my mind but pop like soap bubbles before they can leave my mouth. Instead, I pull back and turn away, looking down at the ground beneath our feet and wondering how it became so cracked and fragile.

He starts again to speak. The words evaporate. He starts again, with a different set of words.

"I haven't stopped looking, Lise ... I look for her every day in every place I go and many I don't. I can't find her. Lise. I think she's gone. I think she's gone." He takes my arm again and forces me to look. "I think she's gone."

There is no sound between us except the deafening silence of all our memories. Our daughter. Seven years old, gone from the fair. A tragedy and another tragedy. The search took us onto the rocks, a party of townsfolk spread out across the Devil's Hand after the tugboat captain thought he'd seen a glimpse of blue, the color of the denim she was wearing. A flash of color through a spyglass that turned out to be nothing but a distraction from his smuggling while the townsfolk looked the other way—who would watch his movements when a child is missing?

Ted Brunel deterred the town with hope and deception and Cora, dear Cora, was swept by a wave, her head smashed on the last of the Hand's fingers, and it was, instead, her body we pulled from the harbour that day, not our child.

Our child has never been found.

Our child has never been found.

I push back my chair, leave Jeremiah sitting there with Ben. I wander about the lighthouse. I touch things. I pick things up, I put them down. I make my way up the spiral to the light room. A bundle of blankets on the floor betrays another of Ben's resting places. I pick up a tattered pillow and breathe it in. Clutching the scent of my husband, I go to the glass and step out onto the balcony. I breathe in the salty air.

Raising the spyglass to my eye, I look out across the rocks where we didn't find our child, but where we watched Cora slip away. I look beyond the rocks now, across the harbour. I find the tiny tugboat, a toy in the spyglass. It bobs angrily on white horses, straining its ropes as if it needs to get away. I focus the circle of my vision through the circle of the porthole, and there, there on a galley shelf, tied around a low wooden rail that keeps things from falling is the very thing that makes me fall.

There, tied to the rail, is a green gingham hair ribbon.

I'll Never Leave You

Alaine Greyson

Jennie Palmer paced the front hallway of her Victorian home. The wood floor creaked with every anxious step. Where was he? Late again. Every few minutes, she pushed the curtains aside and gazed onto the front lawn. Nothing. She checked her phone for a text. Nothing. This was becoming a daily thing.

Like so many boyfriends before, Seth Collins kept her waiting without any explanation. But Jennie understood. She dated important men—men with jobs and friends. She couldn't expect them to drop everything for her. Well, not yet. There would be time for that. Later.

Jennie gazed at her phone then stared out the window at the darkened sky. She hoped Seth arrived before the coming storm. A lone crow perched on the mailbox. Jennie smiled and nodded as it continued its watch. The crow cawed to its murder as they echoed back. Jennie marveled at the sound but was soon interrupted.

Reagan Miles, her best friend and housemate, stood in the hallway with a bowl of ice cream. She leaned against the wall, the spoon halfway in her mouth. "Why do you put up with this? He's late every day. He doesn't text. It's rude."

Jennie sighed. Seth was the latest in a string of boyfriends, but he was different. Jennie had decided he was the one. Well, there had been others she had thought were the one. But Seth … for the first time, Jennie was convinced he would never leave her like the others. He would stay. "It's a quirk I can live with."

"A quirk? He has no respect for you or your time. I don't know what you see in him. Just another in a long line of losers."

Jennie turned toward Reagan, her eyes wide. "He's not a loser. He's just busy, that's all. Besides, he hasn't stood me up."

Reagan huffed. "Yet."

Jennie pursed her lips then turned toward the front door. Reagan never liked any of Jennie's boyfriends. It bothered her, but Jennie chalked it up to jealousy and tried to ignore her.

"You've been with Seth for how long?"

"Three months."

Reagan smirked. "Longer than most. He'll end up with the others soon. You have to choose better next time."

"There won't be a next time."

Reagan chuckled then strolled down the hallway toward the living room.

For once, Jennie wanted Reagan to support her choices. Every time she introduced Reagan to someone new, she found faults she would broadcast. Every relationship she had, Reagan found a way to sabotage. But so far, Seth was immune to Reagan. That's why he had to be the one. If Seth could stand up to Reagan and not fall for her games, then they could be together. Her search for the perfect mate could stop. Seth wouldn't end up like the others. Jennie would ensure it.

A knock at the door startled her. Finally. Jennie opened the door, a wide smile growing across her face. "Where have you been?"

Seth held up his hand. "Don't start. You knew I'd come when I could."

Jennie nodded. "Yes, I know. Well, what are we doing?"

Seth stepped inside and wiped his shoes on the doormat. "I've had a long day. Why don't you make me some dinner, and I'll relax in front of the television?"

Jennie gazed at the floor. "Yes, Seth. Anything particular?"

Seth cupped her face with his hand. "Whatever you want. Surprise me."

Jennie nodded and walked toward the kitchen. She smoothed her skirt, her hopes for the evening dashed. While she loved spending any time she could with Seth, she was looking forward to going out to dinner—something romantic and fancy. But Seth wasn't the romantic or fancy type. At least she was spending the evening with him.

Before reaching the kitchen, a scream interrupted her thoughts. Jennie turned on her heel and stared at the basement door which stood in the hallway leading to the living room.

Reagan leaned on the doorframe, her gaze fixed on Seth. "Basement is off limits."

Seth gulped. "Hiding something, you little witch?"

Reagan laughed. "Witch, huh? You have no idea."

"Stop. Leave my man alone." Jennie stepped between them and grabbed Seth's arm. "I have a lasagna I can heat up. Will that work?"

"Lasagna is fine. Reagan—she's kinda scaring me."

Jennie wrinkled her nose. "Scaring you how? You mean that little act she put on in the hallway? Ignore her."

"She's hard to ignore. Does she always stare at people like she wants to eat them?"

Jennie chuckled. "Eat them? Where are you getting that? I mean, Reagan's not your biggest fan, but she doesn't want to eat you."

Seth approached her and wrapped his arms around her waist. He nuzzled his face into her neck and nibbled. "If it's all the same to you, I'll stay in here and watch you cook. It's safer. And more fun."

Jennie wrapped her arms around him and placed her head on his shoulder. "I'm glad you're here, and I'm glad we stayed in. Never leave?"

"I'm not going anywhere."

For once, Jennie felt secure. Seth wasn't like her other boyfriends—run off by Reagan. Even though she scared him, Seth stayed close to Jennie. She was safe and secure with him, leaning on his promises.

For the next thirty minutes, Jennie scurried around the kitchen, preparing their meal, while Seth watched from the small island. She felt like a dutiful housewife making dinner for her man. It pleased Seth, so it pleased her.

"How about some garlic bread with that lasagna?" Seth leaned his elbows on the island and grinned.

Jennie turned toward him and smiled. "Sure thing." Her smile faded when Reagan popped her head into the kitchen. *Why couldn't she go to the basement and play with her toys or something?* Jennie tilted her head and motioned to the basement door.

"Everything okay?" Seth shot her a confused look.

"Yes. Everything is fine."

"Fine, is it? Or will it only be fine if I go to the basement? Am I bothering your date, Jennie?" Reagan sidled up to Seth and placed her hand on his shoulder. "Do I scare you, lover boy?"

Seth turned and gazed in her eyes. "Should you? I mean, can you? I admit you're a little creepy, but scared? Not so much."

Reagan laughed. "We'll see." She strode toward Jennie and peeked in the pot simmering on the stove. Reagan dipped a finger in the pot and licked it. "Sauce?"

"Of course. What else did you expect?"

"Oh, I don't know." Reagan cocked her head toward Seth, her eyes dancing with mischief. "Blood?" She cackled and strolled toward Seth. "I'm kidding."

Jennie shook her head. Yet another example of Reagan's lack of trust. What else would she make besides sauce for the lasagna?

Reagan removed a container from the refrigerator. "How adventurous are you, Seth? Care to try some of this?" She peeled off the lid and shoved the container in his face ... "It's quite pungent, isn't it?"

"Is that fancy talk for it stinks?"

Jennie rolled her eyes. "Get that rat carcass out of my kitchen. I'm sure Cleo is hungry. Go feed your pet and leave us alone."

Seth's gaze followed Reagan out of the kitchen and toward the basement door. "Rat carcass? In your refrigerator?"

Jennie shrugged. "Our pets have very particular pallets."

Seth shook his head and plopped onto a bar stool. "Visits here are never boring." Jennie was glad for that. If he was never bored, he'd never leave—even if Reagan tried to scare him away. "Dinner's up."

THE NEXT FEW WEEKS, Jennie and Seth planned dates away from the house and away from Reagan. Seth assured her Reagan didn't scare him, but Jennie wasn't taking any chances. She wouldn't lose another boyfriend because of Reagan's games.

This evening, Jennie chose the park for their date—a quiet picnic next to the lake with no Reagan or rat carcasses to interrupt. Jennie picked a secluded spot under a tall maple tree and spread out the red-checkered blanket. As she unloaded the picnic basket and set a place setting for each of them, a shadow fell over the ground.

"Here you are. I was wondering where you disappeared to. What's with all the fancy dishes? Special occasion?"

Reagan. "What are you doing here, and how did you find me?"

"I have my ways." Reagan plopped on the blanket and sorted through the food containers. "Sandwiches and chocolate. Interesting combination. I thought you'd serve something a bit more sophisticated, like cheesecake and strawberry sauce. After all, you want to keep Seth, don't you?"

Jennie grabbed the container from Reagan and pouted. Reagan didn't need to know the menu or the meaning behind it. She knew what she was about, and everything would go smoothly if Reagan didn't interfere. "Of course, I want to keep Seth. That's why we're not meeting at the house anymore. So you can't scare him away. Be good to me and leave."

"Nope. I'm not letting you repeat your mistakes. If you keep going, Seth will end up like the rest of your boyfriends, and you'll be alone and miserable. He's not the one for you, Jennie."

"You have no right to judge. How do you know he's not right for me? He's not scared of you."

"Yet you still want to hide him from me. I'm worried about you, Jennie. You get wrapped up in these guys, and when it doesn't work out ..."

Jennie placed her hands on her hips and scowled. "It doesn't work out because of you. It's all because of you, Reagan. Every relationship I'm ever in, you sabotage until the guy runs screaming from our house. They all leave me because of you."

Reagan softened her gaze. "That's not how I remember it, but, if you think it's all because of me, you're more damaged than I thought."

Jennie broke eye contact to survey the parking lot. "Seth's here. Please leave us alone."

Reagan nodded. "This conversation isn't over. I'm not letting you self-destruct, like you always do. And you will want to self-destruct, because he's not the one."

As Reagan walked away, Jennie rubbed her eyes and straightened her dress. What did Reagan know, anyway? Seth was the one. He had promised he'd never leave, and Jennie believed him. She wouldn't self-destruct, and Seth wouldn't end up like the others. Why did Reagan have so little faith in her?

"Nice set up. What's on the menu?"

Jennie startled. "Seth, I'm still getting everything prepared."

Seth sat cross-legged on the blanket and examined the containers. "Sandwiches?" He picked one up and sniffed. "Interesting smell. What are the ingredients this time?"

"Nothing special. Just liver and dandelion jelly."

He wrinkled his nose. "Liver? I suppose that's better than rat carcass."

"You'd be surprised how delicious rat can be, if seasoned properly."

Seth chuckled. "You're joking, right?"

Jennie sat next to Seth and snuggled into his chest. "We've been seeing each other for almost four months. You've made me very happy. Do I make you happy?"

Seth cleared his throat and pushed her away. "Sure, I'm happy." He reached for the picnic basket and rummaged through the containers. "Anything else in here besides liver?"

Jennie huffed. "I'm trying to talk to you about us. We can eat later."

"Well, you know the way to a man's heart and all ..."

"I'm trying to tell you that I love you."

Seth exhaled and ran his fingers through his hair. "Jennie, like you said, it's been about four months ..."

"Yes?"

"And, well. I like you."

But he doesn't love me. Jennie knew the drill. She gave her heart often and fast. But her feelings were rarely returned. She attracted them long enough for a few months of fun, but, when she confessed her love ...

"I'm not saying I couldn't love you. It's too soon. Can't we just enjoy a nice picnic, enjoy the conversation instead of focusing on the heavy stuff? I want to have fun." Seth pushed back a lock of her hair. "I like being with you. Isn't that enough?"

Jennie smiled. "I'm sorry. Of course, it's enough." She retrieved a container and a fork from the picnic basket. "Here, let's start with dessert. My famous cheesecake with strawberry sauce." She opened the lid and filled the fork. "You'll love this. It'll make the liver go down nice and easy."

Seth cocked his head. "No special ingredients? You didn't substitute cat piss for butter, did you?"

Jennie cackled. "Silly! Why would I do that? Come on, open wide. This is a family recipe, and I know you'll like it." Everyone liked her cheesecake. It had been passed down through generations. Jennie remembered the stories her mother and grandmother told of how they got their husbands to fall in love with them. Every story involved the special cheesecake. If it worked for them, it had to work for her. Eventually. She fed Seth a spoonful, the strawberry sauce oozing over the cheesecake and down the fork.

Strawberry sauce ran down Seth's chin.

Jennie scraped it with the fork and deposited it his mouth. "Lick the fork and get every last drop. Don't want that sugary goodness to go to waste, do you?"

Seth licked his lips then reached for Jennie. "Come here, my love. I want to hold you and watch the sunset. Although, it has nothing on your beauty."

Jennie grinned. This was the Seth she wanted, the Seth Reagan didn't want her to have. But Jennie needed him. She needed his unconditional, unending love, and, if this was the way to get it, Reagan didn't need to know she brought her special dessert. Sometimes love required desperate measures. No one left after they tasted her cheesecake and special strawberry sauce. Not even Seth Collins.

JENNIE CREPT down the basement steps, following the mewing sound of Reagan's cats. The lights were dim, and a musty smell filled the room. Last year, a water pipe had burst and left the basement damp and moldy. They hadn't the funds to fix it yet, so they had to make do. With each step, the stairs creaked, giving warning of her arrival.

"If you're coming down, you better have food." Reagan stood in the corner, thumbing through a book, while a herd of cats mewed about the floor.

"There's plenty. Sometimes I think they wouldn't eat if I didn't bring food down every night." Jennie placed a bag on a table in the center of the basement. "Come here, Cleo. And bring your crew too. I have plenty of food to go around."

The cats leapt onto the table and sniffed at the bag. They pawed each container as Jennie peeled off the lid and set it in front of them.

"So, your picnic with Seth. It went well?"

Jennie flashed a wide grin. "Yes. It was perfect."

Reagan closed the book and folded her arms. "Perfect? He liked the liver?"

"The liver, not so much. But he enjoyed the dessert."

"The chocolates? They didn't seem so … out of the ordinary."

Jennie stroked Cleo's back, flashing Reagan a mischievous grin. "Oh, the chocolates weren't dessert."

Reagan's eyes bulged as a cawing sound emanated from the opposite side of the room. She strode toward Jennie but stopped when a door closed, and the stairs creaked. "Did you leave the front door unlocked? You know that's the first rule. Lock the front door when we're in the basement."

Jennie craned her neck and glanced at their guest. "Seth! It's okay, Reagan. It's just Seth."

"Jennie, he shouldn't be here. It's not safe, or wise."

"It's okay. I didn't tell you, but we had cheesecake for dessert this evening. Well, Seth had cheesecake with a heaping forkful of strawberry sauce."

Reagan pursed her lips. "You did it, even though I warned you? After everything I said last time, you still decided to do it again?"

Jennie marched toward Seth and wrapped her arm around his shoulders. She guided him toward Reagan and met her gaze. "He loves me. Don't you, Seth? Tell Reagan how beautiful I am compared to the sunset."

Seth grabbed Jennie's hips and pulled her close. "Beautiful, like the sunset. I love you, Jennie." His mouth met hers in a deep kiss, their tongues tangling.

"Stop. This ends." Reagan shoved a glass of clear liquid in Seth's hand. "Drink."

Jennie's face reddened as her eyes grew round. "How dare you interfere again! I love him, and he loves me."

"Thanks to the strawberry sauce. He doesn't love you, Jennie. I told you he wasn't the one."

Seth plunked the glass on the table and gazed around the room. "Where am I?"

"You're here with me, my love."

Seth wrinkled his forehead. "Love? Jennie? I thought we talked about this."

Jennie ran her fingers through his hair. "It's okay. I'll take good care of you, forever. You'll never leave me, right?"

As Jennie stroked his head, spider webs formed around his shoulders and torso, wrapping him like Saran Wrap. "What are you doing? How can this be happening?"

"Don't be afraid. We'll have the perfect life together. You'll never want for anything."

"Except his freedom." Reagan stood behind Jennie, her arms outstretched. "Let him go. This isn't the way to get a mate."

Jennie turned and glared into Reagan's eyes. "You keep

telling me he'll end up like the rest. If he does, it's on you. Leave us alone, and he'll be fine."

"Fine? Captured and forced to live with you is fine? Set him free, Jennie."

"No." Jennie faced Seth. "He's mine, and I'm not giving him up."

"Then I have no choice." With a flick of her wrist, Reagan threw Jennie across the room then sliced through the spider webs, freeing Seth.

"Don't just stand there. Run!" Reagan pushed Seth toward the steps.

"I don't understand."

"She's trying to separate us, my love." Jennie strode toward Seth.

He shifted his gaze from Reagan to Jennie. "Perhaps I should go."

"Go? We made a promise to be together forever."

Seth rubbed his forehead. "I don't remember making a promise. I said I just wanted to have fun. With all respect, this is kinda spooky, not fun. What are you girls anyway? Witches?"

Reagan smirked. "You could say that. Now don't be stupid, and run."

Seth placed a foot on the bottom step, and a gust of wind threw him on the floor. "What the …?"

"I said you weren't leaving me."

Reagan waved her arms, lifted Jennie in the air and deposited her on the table. "Remember last time? And the times before? I knew he'd end up like the others. It's not because of me. I'm not the one forcing them to stay. It always ends badly. I can't let you do this again."

"Stop me." As her anger grew, Jennie's body towered over Reagan. She raised her arms as a murder of crows cawed around her. "I get what I want. They never leave, do they Reagan?" Light emanated from Jennie's fingers and shone around the dank room. Skeletons, random bones, and skulls lined the walls.

"You want love? A pile of bones can't love you."

"I want commitment, loyalty, never-ending devotion."

"And they give that to you?"

Jennie grasped Reagan's shoulders and gazed into her eyes. "In life, they had freewill. Now their only will is to serve me." Jennie shone a light on the bones as they jostled and formed a line in front of her.

"Do you want this war?"

"War? There's no war. There's only me getting what I want while you watch, helpless."

Reagan extended her hand, pushing Jennie toward the bones.

The pile formed a chair and caught Jennie before she hit the floor. "They're on my side. They'll always protect me."

"So you say. Witch to witch, you only have your spells to guarantee their loyalty."

"Does it matter? They obey my every whim. That's more than I can ever say for you. You never listened. You never understood." A skeleton approached Jennie and wrapped bony arms around her shoulders. She nestled into its chest and stroked its arm. "They listen. They love me and will never leave."

"They can't leave."

"Enough." Jennie stood, and the bone chair dismantled and hung in the air. "Stop wasting my time. No more interference." With a nod, the bones flew toward Reagan and formed a circle around her.

"Let me out. This isn't right."

"You didn't complain this much with the others."

Reagan shook the bone cage and scowled. "It wouldn't have mattered."

"Then why does it matter now?" Jennie ran her finger down the bone jail. "If you let me use my powers the way they were intended—"

"Our powers are not meant to kill or trap people. You want love? Forcing someone to stay isn't love. Casting a spell and kidnapping them isn't love. And killing them to keep them isn't love."

Jennie stooped and met Reagan's gaze. "What do you know? Who do you love, except for your stupid cats? No, I know what love is. And I will do whatever I must to keep it." Jennie turned and gazed on the skeletons surrounding Seth. "My skeleton friends were once like you. They wanted to leave, but now they answer to my commands. Care to join them? Either way, you're not leaving. No one leaves me."

Seth scrambled to his knees and crawled toward the wall.

Jennie followed, her pet crows trailing behind her.

"Get away. Call off your friends and let me leave."

"My friends? You haven't seen what I'm capable of yet." Jennie drew a fiery circle in the air and cast it on the walls. More skeletons stirred and righted themselves, forming an army at Jennie's disposal. "Think you can escape? That's what these poor souls thought too. No one leaves Jennie Palmer."

Seth crawled toward the stairs and heaved himself onto the bottom step. "You're crazy. And neither you, your crow friends, or that pile of bones can keep me here."

"Really?" Jennie nodded as the three skeletons scaled the stairs and blocked his exit. Two more grabbed his arms and pinned him against the wall.

Seth closed his eyes. "This is just a dream. It isn't real."

"Oh, but it is. You could have prevented all this"

"How? You're unhinged. And these skeletons, they were once alive?"

"They, too, had a choice. But they chose wrong. Don't repeat their mistakes."

Seth glanced at the staircase. "Help! Someone has to hear."

Jennie cackled. "No one can hear you. We soundproofed the basement years ago. I'm not stupid."

Seth kicked both skeletons, causing them to tumble in a pile on the floor. He ran toward the staircase only for Jennie's pets to halt him.

"You're not comprehending. Either you marry me or my crow friends murder you." Jennie tilted her head back and cackled. "Get it? Murdered by a murder of crows? That never gets old."

Seth covered his face with his hands. "I'll never marry you."

"Very well." Jennie strolled toward the table.

"That's it? I can go?"

Jennie gazed into his eyes as she raised her arms. "Yes. You can go." She lowered her arms as her crows sped toward Seth. "To the afterlife."

The crow's caws and Seth's screams intermingled, creating an eerie sound Jennie found pleasing and comforting. She was joined with Seth for eternity. Reagan had failed, and once again, Jennie had won. She flashed Reagan a satisfied smile. "You didn't put up much of a fight this time. Are you weak or tired?"

Reagan huffed and turned toward the back of the basement.

Jennie cradled a skull in her arms and surveyed the carnage. Her crows were efficient. By morning, his bones would be picked clean, leaving little for her to tidy. Then Seth could join her skeleton crew, ready to serve forever.

As she watched her darlings pick at the carcass that had once been her love, she stroked the skull and smiled. "In the end, you'll never leave me. None of them ever do."

Jennie strolled toward the door, pleased with her days work. As she placed her hand on the railing, a cold air breezed past her shoulders. She glanced at the half-flesh, half-bone hand outstretched toward her. As she turned, an army of skeletons, led by Seth, approached.

In unison they chanted, "Jennie, never leave us."

Reagan floated above the scene, directing the crows. "I'm granting your wish. Now they'll never leave you, and you'll never leave us. Obsession gets its just rewards."

Death at the Masquerade

Alaine Greyson

S ecrets destroyed lives. Millie Jones knew this well. But here she was, in Evelyn Taylor's bedroom, listening to the latest confidence she was charged to keep and wishing Evelyn would choose another friend to share her secrets.

"Edward doesn't want anyone to know, so you can't tell a soul. Not your mother, your sister, or even Claudia." Evelyn flitted around the bedroom like a busy butterfly, arranging her outfit for the evening festivities.

It was almost Halloween, and Edward Bennett had invited the entire town of Kinney to a masquerade ball. Keeping a secret at an event where the whole town was gathered would be near impossible, especially given the Kinney's size. Founded in the 1700s, Kinney's residents were few, comprised mainly of the founding families. Newcomers weren't common and were regarded as suspect. Edward included. Millie didn't trust Edward, but she didn't share her view with Evelyn. It would be nice if she could share this burden.

"Claudia won't like being left out." Since they were in

grade school, Millie, Evelyn and Claudia were inseparable. They went through every phase of life together, from the awkward pre-teen years to the career women they were today. It was odd that Evelyn would exclude Claudia, but, with Evelyn, there was always an explanation.

"Claudia doesn't like Edward. She wouldn't understand, and I don't want to argue with her. When Edward is ready to announce it to the world, I'll make sure Claudia isn't blindsided. But, for now, we keep it between you and me … and Edward."

Millie stood and strolled toward the closet, running her fingers down a red velvet dress. "I don't understand why it's a secret. Who are you hiding from?"

Evelyn shrugged. "Edward says he wants to announce our relationship properly. He wants to squash any rumors."

"Rumors? Do you think people will talk trash about you? About Claudia, yes. But you? If anyone has rumors swirling around, it's Edward himself. Waltzing into town and buying that abandoned mansion, no one knowing who he is or where he came from, that's where the rumors start."

"Everyone is entitled to their past. I don't know why it matters. Edward is a perfect gentleman, so kind and loving."

Millie rolled her eyes. This wasn't the first time Evelyn had fallen in love. Whenever she fell for a new guy, it was hard and fast. Millie and Claudia did their best to listen and stand by her, because they knew the relationship would explode. At some point, the guy didn't meet Evelyn's expectations, or he broke it off because Evelyn became too obsessive. Whatever the reason, Millie knew she had to stick close and help her pick up the pieces when this current infatuation fell apart. "Can I borrow this tonight?"

Evelyn grabbed the dress and held it against Millie. "I

think this is perfect. But you need a mask to match. After all, Edward's party is a masquerade." Evelyn sorted through her top dresser drawer and removed a red feather mask. "Here. This will complete the look and cause all the men to stop in their tracks."

Millie took the mask and scrunched her nose. "It's not too much? I mean, the dress is kind of ..."

"Sexy? Come on, Millie. Loosen up a bit. You'll never find a guy if you cover up everything. Show a little skin and flirt for a change. You might enjoy it."

Millie sighed. Getting a man was never high on her list. It was more important to grow her career. If she played it right, she could have the corner office in her advertising company within the next five years. That left little time for flirting.

"Get changed. We're picking up Claudia in an hour. And remember, not a word to anyone until Edward is ready to announce it. I don't want to disappoint him."

Evelyn disappeared into the bathroom, leaving Millie to contemplate the night ahead. Keeping Evelyn's secret would be easy if Evelyn cooperated. But this was seldom the case. How could she keep Evelyn's secret when it was written all over her face?

Keeping the secret was only one problem she faced tonight. The masquerade ball itself posed its own problems. By nature, Millie was an introvert. She didn't like wild parties and socializing, like Claudia. She didn't have a man like Edward to distract her. So why was she willing to wear a dress that would draw attention? If she was to keep the secret, shouldn't she wear something demure?

Millie unbuttoned her pants and let them fall to the floor. She slipped out of her blouse and gazed at the bed, the red velvet dress staring back. This was the dress she longed to wear but never had the courage. Did she dare? She ran her fingers down the length of the dress, remembering how alluring it had looked on Evelyn. Millie couldn't do it justice, could she? She held the dress to her body. She wasn't skinny like Evelyn or curvy like Claudia. A more conservative dress would better suit.

"You're not changing your mind. Put on that dress, trust me."

Millie glanced toward the bathroom door. "You wear it."

Evelyn pulled out a midnight blue dress with azure chiffon fabric draping the back like a train. Tiny jewels that sparkled when they caught the light covered the chiffon fabric, making the dress seem like it was caught in the moonlight. "This is a gift from Edward. He wanted me to shine tonight. All eyes will be on me."

Millie huffed. "And all eyes will discover your secret."

"Not if you don't tell."

"I have no plans on telling. Your face, on the other hand … You might want to have a discussion with it."

Evelyn laughed. "Think I'll reveal my own secret? Doubtful. Edward is far too important for anything to mess this up. I'll keep close to you and Claudia until he's ready to reveal our relationship. I'm sure he's planning something special tonight. Why else have a ball? He'll make an announcement at the end, and we can all toast our happiness."

Millie sighed. She hoped Evelyn was right and the night went like her friend planned, but she had an uncomfortable feeling in the pit of her stomach. Something wasn't right about Edward. She vowed to stick close to Evelyn in case she had to pick up the pieces once again.

MILLIE STEPPED onto the cobblestone path leading toward Edward's mansion. She gazed at the unmanicured lawn, wondering why Edward didn't bother to tidy the place before the ball. The grass and weeds overtook the front yard, spilling over the stone walkway that led to the front door. The mansion had been abandoned for years before Edward bought it six months prior. Millie wondered why he hadn't begun renovations. The windows were old, and the gray shutters hung crooked on their hinges. The house was painted a dingy brown and looked almost black with the years of mold and soot. It reminded Millie of a horror film. She hoped the inside was better kept.

Claudia saddled up to Millie and linked arms. "Creepy, huh? You'd think he'd hire a lawn service before a party like this."

"Maybe he thinks it lends to the atmosphere. Masquerades are known to be spooky."

Claudia laughed. "I suppose." She smoothed her dress and ran her fingers through her long auburn hair. "But I'm not here for the scare. I'm hoping to score a few dates tonight. I need some new players. The ones on my current list have lost their sparkle."

Millie sighed. Evelyn fell in love too easily, and Claudia ran from love. What a threesome they made. "I'm just here to watch the two of you and clean up whatever mess is left at the end."

Evelyn joined them on the path and linked her arm with Millie's, the three of them forming an impenetrable line. "There won't be a mess. Tonight will be magical, just wait." Evelyn turned her head and winked. "And, Millie, you might meet your dream man tonight. In that red dress, you'll stop them all in their tracks. Then you can have your pick."

"Hey! Not until I have my chance with them. Millie's never interested in guys at these parties anyway."

"So, I can have your leftovers. Is that what you're saying?"

Claudia tossed back her hair and huffed. "Not at all. You may look alluring in that dress, but guys always flock to me first. I'll snuff them out and send the best ones your way."

Millie pursed her lips. "How kind of you."

"Of course. The three of us stick together, don't we? I have your back."

Claudia had her back. The words amused Millie. Claudia wasn't the altruistic type. She would claim the best for herself and send Millie the rejects. Good thing Millie wasn't interested. If anything, she could help Claudia's failed beaus feel better after being tossed aside for someone more ... successful.

"Edward cleaned up the inside, right? I mean, I get the ambience and everything, but we're not walking into a dilapidated building, are we?" Claudia wrinkled her nose.

Evelyn glanced at Millie, her eyes wide. "How would I know?"

"No offense, but I've seen you cozy up to him."

Millie rolled her eyes. "Evelyn flirts with every guy she meets, much like you. Besides, why would someone as mysterious as him be interested in Evelyn when you're hanging around?" Millie tilted her head and winked at Evelyn.

Claudia tossed back her hair and smiled. "True. Nonetheless, this party better be everything I'm expecting. Spooky is fine, but dirty and dangerous? I'll pass."

"Don't worry. Everything will be perfect, and we'll

have the best night. I'm sure Edward took every pain to ensure his guests are satisfied. After all, this is his chance to ingratiate himself with the town. I don't think he'd risk anything bad happening at his first party." Evelyn tightened her grip on Millie's arm and trudged toward the front door.

The trio approached the mansion, surrounded by other townspeople anxious to discover the state of the ancient building. The mansion was a mainstay, a relic of the towns founding hundreds of years ago. But few had entered in decades since the last owner died. The outside showed its neglect and added a spooky factor, lending the mansion to rumors about ghostly beings and strange happenings.

Millie shivered. The fall night air was cool, and her dress wasn't enough to warm her. She should have chosen a more conservative outfit. It was too late now. She was committed to this night, this outfit, and this secret. She gazed at the full moon that cast an eerie light over the property. Was a full moon the night of a masquerade ball a lucky sign? Millie unhooked her arms and straightened her dress.

"Nervous? Don't worry, I have your back. Just follow my lead." Claudia grasped the oversized black door knocker and banged.

An attractive man in a black tuxedo answered. "Ladies, Mr. Bennet is expecting you. This way to the ballroom."

Evelyn turned toward Claudia and smiled. "See? Nothing to worry about."

The trio followed their guide, with other townspeople close behind, toward the back of the residence. Millie hung onto Evelyn's arm as they strode down the hallway, wary of the spiderwebs, swords, and knights' armor that lined the walls. Millie gazed at the armor and dug her fingers into Evelyn's arm.

"Ouch! What was that for?"

Millie's face turned ashen. "That armor. I'm sure it moved. I think it's watching us."

Evelyn wrestled her arm from Millie's grasp. "You're imagining things. Armor can't move on its own. Stop trying to scare us."

"I'm not trying to scare anyone. I just have an awful feeling in the pit of my stomach."

Evelyn glanced at Claudia, who was flirting with their guide, then pulled Millie to the side. "Whatever you think is happening, it isn't. Everything is fine. You will keep my secret, and you will make sure tonight goes well. I need this, Millie."

Millie sighed. This was why she didn't like getting involved with Evelyn's love affairs. They were always do or die, and they always inconvenienced Millie. But she had given her word. "Okay. I'll keep my promise."

Evelyn smiled. "Good."

Resigned to her fate, Millie pushed the thought of the moving armor from her mind, blaming it on an overactive imagination. She strode into the ballroom behind their guide and beheld the sparsely decorated room. Cobwebs hung from the ceiling. A table full of appetizers and punch lay to one side. The remainder of the room was empty. Millie assumed on purpose for the dancing. It didn't look like any ball she'd ever attended. But then Edward Bennet wasn't like any man she'd ever known.

"Mr. Bennet will be with you soon. Please, partake of a refreshment or two." And, with that, their guide disappeared.

"Is this on purpose, or is he too cheap to fix the place?"

"Claudia, relax. It's fine. It's supposed to be spooky, remember?" Evelyn strolled toward the middle of the dance floor and twirled, her dress flowing around her. "I can't wait for the dancing. Tonight will be magical, just wait."

Millie crossed her arms and surveyed the room. "If you say so. Something doesn't feel right. I get the spooky factor, but there's more to it."

Evelyn shot Millie a menacing glance. "You promised."

Yes, she had promised. And now she regretted it. If they survived the night, this would be the last promise and secret she would ever keep for Evelyn. The cost was too high.

Millie meandered toward the refreshments table. Two women she recognized from the local library stood next to the punch bowl. Millie glanced at the food options while she eavesdropped on their conversation.

"This place is so medieval. If he was going for that, he succeeded." Bernice, the taller of the two, leaned toward her companion. "Did you see the knights' armor in the hallway? So authentic."

"Well, he must have ran out of money, because this room is lacking atmosphere. The cobwebs add a spooky element, but he could have had a spider or a skeleton or something. It's disappointing."

Millie recognized the second woman as Janet, the town's biggest gossip—the one person who could ruin Evelyn if she discovered the secret. Millie chose a brownie, placed it on a plate and turned toward Claudia.

"Millie Robbins? Is that you?"

Crap. Millie froze and drew a breath. Then she plastered a smile on her face and turned on her heel. "Janet. How nice to see you. I was grabbing Claudia a bit of dessert, so if you'll excuse me."

Janet latched onto Millie's elbow and pulled. "That can wait. Let's hear your opinion. Do you think Edward decorated well for the occasion, or do you think the lack of decoration signals that he's broke?"

"I'm not his accountant."

Bernice chuckled. "Of course not, dear. You can still have an opinion. What do you think of Edward? He's a bit strange."

"Strange? The man is a recluse. I never see him around town. It was a shock to receive our invitation, but we had to know," Janet said

Millie scrunched her eyes. "Know what?"

"The secret, my dear. There is a secret. Edward is far too mysterious to not have a hidden past or motives. Why did he move here and buy this old mansion? And why hasn't he renovated it? Don't you find it odd?"

Millie did find it odd, but she couldn't have these old biddies investigating and discovering Evelyn's secret—at least not until Edward gave the okay; although Millie still didn't understand what the fuss was about. So Evelyn and Edward were an item. Why the mystery? "Not particularly. You know the rich, always eccentric. That's all it is, nothing so ominous as you're suggesting."

Bernice smirked then latched onto Janet's arm.

Millie jolted when the lights flickered, and a deep groan shook the room.

"What was that?" Janet stammered.

Millie inhaled and composed herself. "Special effects. See? That's where the money went. Who needs fancy decorations when you have flickering lights and moaning on cue? I think Edward did a fine job, don't you?" Millie flashed a smile and waltzed toward Claudia. She would have to keep Evelyn away from Bernice and Janet's prying.

Sound effects. Millie shook her head. She wasn't sure if Bernice and Janet bought her explanation. She hoped it was convincing enough, since Millie didn't believe it herself. Something wasn't right, and it was bigger than Evelyn's secret.

Millie glanced toward the middle of the room where Claudia was holding court. Like always, the most successful and gorgeous men in the room surrounded her. And like always, she appeared confident and alluring. Millie didn't know how she did it. As she tried to sneak past the crowd, Claudia caught her gaze and motioned her to join. Millie exhaled. She would have to face this sometime.

"Millie! We were just talking about you, weren't we, fellas?"

The men plastered a smile on their faces and nodded in unison.

Claudia placed an arm around Millie and whispered, "Follow my lead." Claudia turned toward her admirers and grinned. "Millie is my oldest and dearest friend. She's a wonderful dancer, so scoop her up when the dancing starts."

The men nodded and mumbled in agreement.

Millie hated being forced on Claudia's fan club. She wanted someone who liked her for who she was, not who she knew. Millie turned to escape Claudia's scheme as the lights flickered off, and a loud boom sounded.

"Now, now. No need to be afraid. It's all a part of the show. Can't have a masquerade at Halloween without special effects, can you?" Edward entered the room, his loud booming voice filling the house. "Welcome to my home. I hope you enjoy the refreshments." He waltzed toward Evelyn and bowed. "Madam, would you do me the honor of a dance?"

Millie's mouth hung open. Edward wasn't hiding his interest in Evelyn. Why was she entrusted with this secret if they couldn't keep their eyes off each other? Janet and Bernice would have rumors spreading before the dance was over. Millie took two steps toward the couple and stopped.

A tall black-haired man placed his hand on her shoulder and turned her toward him. "Would you care to dance?"

Great. Claudia had foisted one of her leftovers on her. How could she get Evelyn alone to talk if she was dancing with this strange, gorgeous man? Well, he was gorgeous. "I don't normally dance with strange men."

He took Millie's hand and bowed. "Let's remedy that. I'm Colin, and you're Millie. Now I'm not so strange. Shall we?"

Millie chuckled. "Since you know my name, you must be one of Claudia's friends."

"Yes. Claudia. Wonderful girl. Enough about her. Let's dance."

Millie allowed Colin to lead her onto the dance floor. She placed one hand on his shoulder and another around his waist. "I haven't seen you around town before."

"I'm visiting. Edward invited some of his friends to attend the party and help him feel more at home."

"Are we not welcoming enough?"

Colin laughed. "You are very welcoming. But sometimes you want a familiar face when you're around new people."

Millie understood. She had known everyone in town her entire life, and she still had problems fitting in. She couldn't imagine how hard it must be for Edward. But at least he had Evelyn.

"Who is Edward dancing with?"

Millie's breath hitched. Colin didn't know Evelyn. That meant Edward hadn't shared their relationship with his friend. "That's my best friend Evelyn."

Colin fixed his gaze on Evelyn. "She's pretty."

Millie exhaled. Was Colin interested in Evelyn? That could cause problems. Millie had to get Evelyn alone after this dance. "How long are you staying in town?"

"Not sure. As long as Edward needs my assistance, I'm here." Colin leaned forward and placed his lips next to Millie's ear. "Longer, if I have a chance to know you better."

Millie blushed. Something felt different about Colin, but she couldn't explain it. His hands were ice cold, and he seemed to float as they danced. The whole thing unnerved her, but she couldn't put it into words. She had to tread carefully and discover what Colin and Edward were really doing in town.

When the dance ended, Colin bowed and retreated to the refreshments table.

Millie rushed toward Evelyn. "What are you doing?"

Evelyn's eyes sparkled. "Having a good time. It looks like you enjoyed that dance as well. He's cute."

Millie pursed her lips. She didn't come here to meet a guy, cute or not. Besides, something was out of place about Colin, and she wasn't interested in exploring a connection. Her focus was on Evelyn and keeping the secret. Something told her it was more important than it seemed. "Cut it out. If you want me to keep your secret, you gotta help. You can't dance and make eyes at Edward like that. Janice and Bernice are probably spreading rumors already. Whatever is going on, you have to stop."

"We had once dance. And look, Edward's making the rounds and flirting with other girls too. No one will give it a second thought."

Millie's gaze shifted toward the refreshment table to see Edward leaning against the table, deep in conversation with Bernice and Janet. *Nice move. It's like he knows.* Millie shook her head. "Just be careful, please? Something isn't right."

"You worry too much." Evelyn hiked her dress and strode toward Claudia.

Millie sighed. Something wasn't right. She felt it in the pit of her stomach. But how could she get anyone to listen? She startled when a voice boomed into her ear, "There's something you're not telling me about your friend."

"Colin. Don't sneak up on me like that."

Colin placed his arms around her and pinned her wrists to her abdomen. "You have to tell me, Millie. What is going on between Edward and your friend?"

Millie gulped. "Why don't you ask Edward?"

"Edward is less than transparent. I'm asking you. Are they involved?"

"Involved? No, of course not. Edward hasn't been in town long enough to date anyone. Besides, he's not big on socializing."

Colin turned Millie toward him. "I'm not playing games. You need to tell me what is going on. It could mean your friend's life."

Millie's face turned ashen. What were Colin and Edward caught up in that would cost Evelyn her life?

"Listen. It's not just Evelyn's life at stake. Everyone here is in grave danger."

"Then why did Edward invite us? Is he aware?"

Colin exhaled. "No. I'm here to protect him … and you."

"From what?"

Millie and Colin jolted when a scream echoed from the balcony. They rushed toward the sound and stopped beside a bereft Claudia.

"We were talking. She wasn't even leaning on the

railing. It's like someone picked her up and threw her over."

Millie glanced over the railing at the woman lying on the ground. "Kristin. We went to school together." A tear streaked her face. "How could this happen?"

Colin gazed at the night sky. "She's here. It's too late. No one is safe."

Millie placed her hands on her hips. "Who is *she*? And what does *she* want?"

"Edward. She wants Edward."

Millie pursed her lips and marched into the ballroom.

"Where are you going?" Colin asked.

"To find Edward. I'm not standing by while some mystery woman kills everyone at the party."

"She's not after everyone. Just the women. This is why I needed to know about Edward and Evelyn."

"I don't understand. Some mystery woman who refuses to show her face wants to murder all the women, and all you're concerned with is Edward and Evelyn?"

Colin shot her an incredulous look. "Um, yeah. You can't connect the dots?"

Millie grasped Colin's hand and trudged toward an empty room off the ballroom. She closed the door and sat on the brown leather couch. "Talk."

Colin paced the room. "What do you want me to say?"

"The truth."

"I'm not sure that's a good idea. Some things are better left unsaid."

"A girl I went to school with just died. Some invisible force threw her off the balcony, and you seem to know who was behind it. Now tell me what we're dealing with, and let's figure out how to stop her."

"There is no stopping her. Once she's enraged, nothing calms her down."

"Who is she?"

Colin's mouth hung open when another scream interrupted them. "Oh no."

"Colin, this is serious."

"She's doing it all over again. Just like in life, her jealousy ruins everything. No one is safe."

Millie wrinkled her nose at Colin's cryptic riddles and ran into the ballroom.

Three knives pinned Janet to the wall—two through her stomach, one through her heart. Blood dripped down the wall and covered the floor.

Bernice held one hand over her mouth and pointed at the wall with the other.

Words appeared next to Janet. *I will have my revenge.*

Millie pointed at Edward and Evelyn. "You. Both of you. In that room right now." She turned toward Colin. "You too. This has to end."

The four marched toward the room, and Millie closed the door behind them.

"Do you think everyone else is safe out there?" Evelyn clasped Edward's hand.

"It doesn't matter where people are. She can get to whoever she wants," Colin said.

"Who is she?" Evelyn's voice shook.

Edward gazed at the floor. "It's my fault. I should have known she'd interfere."

"I warned you. Gwen won't leave you alone until you settle things with her. Running away won't solve anything," Colin said.

Evelyn released Edward's hand. "Who's Gwen?"

A cackling sound emanated from the ballroom. The door flung open, and a waft of cold air blew through, whispering, *"Yes, Edward. Do tell. Who is Gwen?"*

Evelyn sank into the cushion and placed her head in

her hands. "She's the reason for the secret. She's the reason you didn't want anyone to know."

A band of smoke floated toward Edward. *"Is she the one you left me for? I thought you'd do better. The other girls were prettier. This one—eh."*

Edward gazed toward the apparition. A blue aura glowed about his face as he stared at the disturbance. "I won't let you have her. And I won't tell you who she is. Her identity will be kept secret."

A disembodied Gwen laughed. *"You want me to believe this little bit, who you are so gallantly protecting, isn't your current mistress? You think me daft?"*

"I think you're crazy, and I refuse to talk to you in this condition. Show yourself."

"Why should I? I've come after her, Edward. And since you won't tell me which one she is, they all die."

"I was tied to you for twenty years in life. I refuse to be tied to you in death. Leave, Gwen. Find another town to haunt."

In death? Was Millie dealing with ghosts? It would explain the strange happenings and why Edward didn't leave the mansion. But could ghosts travel from place to place? Weren't they confined to where they had died? Millie had more questions than answers, but right now, she had to stop Gwen.

Colin placed his hand on Millie's shoulder. "Let's go, while she's distracted. I can get you to safety."

"What about the others?"

"We can't risk it. I can sneak you out, but a mass exodus would only increase her ire."

Millie gazed into Colin's eyes. "You're a ghost too, aren't you?"

"Guilty. Are you disappointed?"

"Confused. I thought ghosts were confined to where

they died."

Colin scratched his head. "Well, some are. There are different types of ghosts. You have your poltergeist, specters, wraiths—"

"I don't need a list. Never mind, you can explain later. Obviously, you can take human form when you need to."

Colin's body faded into a funnel of blue smoke, revealing a skeletal creature dressed in clothes from a time long ago. "Do you prefer me like this?"

Millie wrinkled her nose. "No. Stop the games, and let's make a plan. There must be a way to stop her."

"Have you ever tried to stop an angry ghost?"

"I've never had the opportunity. But my friend's life is in danger."

"Everyone's life is in danger. She won't stop until she eliminates all the competition. Unless …"

"Unless what?"

"Reveal the secret."

Millie placed her hands on her hips and met Colin's gaze. "No. I promised."

"Is keeping the secret worth people's lives?"

"It's worth Evelyn's life. If I reveal the secret, Gwen will kill her."

"I hate to burst your bubble, but Gwen will kill her anyway. And any other female at this party. You have to think of the greater good."

The greater good. Millie shook her head. There was still a chance to escape. While Gwen and Edward argued, she could get the rest of the women out of the mansion and away from Gwen's wrath.

Millie strode toward Evelyn and met her gaze. "We have to get out of here, but I need to know one thing. Did you know Edward was a ghost?"

Evelyn hung her head. "Yes. Didn't you ever wonder

why he couldn't leave the mansion? Why no one saw him around town? I figured it out. But I love him anyway."

"Is love worth all this? Is it worth dying for?"

"You've never fallen in love before, so you don't know what it's like. He's it for me, Millie."

She had never fallen in love before, that was true. But was love between a human and ghost even possible? And, if it was possible, was it more important than the lives of the people at the party? Millie grasped Evelyn's hand and ran from the room. "We have to leave. Get Claudia and Bernice and—"

When they reached the ballroom, Evelyn's face turned white. "Millie …"

In the middle of the room, Claudia and Bernice hung from the ceiling, a rope tied around their necks.

Millie stared at the lifeless bodies dangling from the rafters. *Not Claudia.* Was the secret worth the death of her friend? Either way, Evelyn would be next if she didn't get them out of there.

"This is all my fault. She's after me, not everyone else. I need to stop her before she kills again."

"I'm not losing you too. Let me get you to safety."

"No. I have to face this. Besides, I'm not leaving Edward."

"Staying with him is a death sentence."

"That may be, but I love him. I'm not leaving."

Millie sighed. Tonight wasn't what she had expected. Not even an hour before, everything was happy and calm. Now Millie and Evelyn were the only two women left, and a ghost they couldn't see were hunting them. Millie reached for Evelyn's hand and dragged her toward the front of the mansion. "I'm not leaving you."

When they reached the front door, blue smoke surrounded them, and a voice boomed, *"Not so fast, hussies.*

One of you has been seeing my Edward. Tell me. Not that it matters, because you'll both be dead."

Millie squared her shoulders and approached the apparition. "I don't know much about ghosts. Explain it to me. Can you travel, or are you confined to this mansion?"

Gwen laughed. *"You can discover that after you join me in the afterlife."*

Millie stroked her chin. "If I join you in this … afterlife, could I haunt the whole town or just this mansion? A girl has to plan."

A cold waft of air entered the hallway, knocking down the knights' armor along the wall. *"You foolish girl. Distracting me so your friend can escape? Is it because she's the one I'm after? No matter. I don't intend to leave either one of you alive."*

"Your death must have been tragic to have so much anger stored inside you. How did it happen? Did it happen here? Is that how Edward came to own this mansion?"

"Edward's family built this mansion centuries ago. It was here we lived and here we died."

"Colin too?"

"You ask too many questions."

Evelyn sighed. "Millie, I already know the story. I just didn't know about Gwen." Evelyn glared at the apparition. "Edward conveniently left her out. Colin and Edward are best friends. They died in a fire at this mansion over a hundred years ago."

"In a fire? All three of them?"

"I know Edward and Colin did."

A voice interrupted. "Gwen started the fire."

"Colin, you've accused me of starting the fire for the past hundred years."

"That's because it's true. Gwen thought Edward had a lover. He kept sneaking away to my side of the mansion. But it wasn't a woman he was meeting. Edward and I were planning a new venture, a business deal that would have earned millions. Until Gwen's jealousy caused her to set fire to the mansion. Funny that she was killed in her own evil plan."

"Edward was cheating on me, I know it."

"He wasn't, Gwen. It's all in your mind."

"He's cheating on me now by seeing that hussy."

Evelyn pushed Millie to the side. "Do you think killing everyone will get him back? Will he want to be with you after what you did?"

A puff of white smoke appeared, and the apparition changed to human form, revealing a woman dressed as if from another time. "What do you know about love? Edward made vows to me. He's mine, and I'm claiming him."

"Vows you made in life. Does that transfer to the afterlife?"

Gwen cackled. "I've tracked Edward through the years. This isn't the first time I've stopped one of his love affairs. He's been dead for one hundred years, yet he still thinks he can fall in love with a live human. What kind of life could either one of you have with a ghost?"

Evelyn glanced toward the balcony and reached for Millie's hand. "Come on, I have a plan."

When they reached the railing, Edward and Colin were waiting. "We can't stop her. We've tried before, but she's too strong."

"So, one female ghost is stronger than two male ghosts?" Millie asked.

"Gwen is angry. Anger makes a ghost mean and strong. We can't combat that."

Evelyn held out a knife and exhaled. "I can."

Millie scrunched her nose. "How can you combat a ghost with a knife?"

"It's not for her." Evelyn raised the knife to her wrist and yelled into the wind, "You can't stop him from loving another ghost!"

"Evelyn, no!" Millie lunged forward but fell on the floor.

"It's the only way. Then I can be with Edward forever, and she can't hurt me. And she can't hurt you."

A tear streaked Millie's face. "I lost Claudia, and now I'm losing you. Who will I have left?"

A strong wind swept across the balcony. The sky darkened as a voice boomed, *"You can't escape me. Edward is mine."*

Evelyn stared skyward. "I make my vow to be Edward's forever. In death, I am his, and he is mine." Evelyn raised the knife to her wrist and cut across. Blood poured as she fainted.

Millie choked back tears as she bent down and held Evelyn's hand. "I hope this is everything you wanted, Evelyn." She watched as a vapor rose from Evelyn's body and joined Edward in the night sky.

They grasped hands, smiled at Millie and faded away.

"What do I do now?"

"Your friends live on, here at the mansion. You could always stay here with me."

Millie blinked, trying to make sense of the night's events. "Stay here?"

"I'd like to get to know you better. How do you feel about dating a hundred-year-old ghost?"

All of her friends had died gruesome deaths tonight, yet Colin could only think of dating her? Ghosts had mixed-up priorities. "You don't have an angry ghost wife or girlfriend, do you?"

Colin smiled. "Not that I remember."

Millie glanced skyward as a mist grew around them.

"They are all here, confined to the mansion like you, Edward, and Gwen, right?"

Colin nodded. "They are safe from Gwen, but you ..."

"She could try to kill me if I stay."

"It's a possibility. As much as I want you to stay, to be safe, you should return to town."

Before tonight, Millie wasn't interested in men. But Colin was different. He could teach her a lot about the paranormal world, and that fascinated her. "I would miss Evelyn and Claudia if I left." Millie glanced around the mansion. "But I do insist on redecorating."

The two meandered toward the ballroom and stopped to see Evelyn and Edward dancing while Janet, Bernice, and Claudia watched. It was a different future than Millie had expected, but at least she was with her friends. And together they would thwart Gwen's schemes, or else Millie would join them. Watching her friends smile, she decided that joining them might not be such an awful idea.

When the Arish Discovered Halloween

Marie McGrath

T he land of Arish nestled into the mountainside, teeming with hills and rocky cliffs. The wind howled over the cliffs and whipped around the homes. The Ari people lived a simple but enchanted life. Magic ensured their survival, but it also enriched it.

"Relic Caligari, what are we doing out here? It is late and chilly. This weather will get someone sick. We should be in our homes," Dante Crypt said as he pulled his overcoat closer to his body. It was unusual for a Proper to be out this late, even with a Relic of the community.

"You are new to being a Proper and have much to learn. I assure you, we do everything for a reason." Relic Caligari moved forward, clutching his crystal. It glowed and emitted immense light for them to see. His crystal was a pale blue and a rare color for one's crystal.

Dante clutched his own crystal—a deep purple—as the magic within focused. It was a witch's or warlock's birthright. Every baby was given their own at birth to harness their magic.

A loud bang rang through the night. Relic Caligari and

Dante both stopped, peering into the distance. The sound came from a home up the street. They hurried along the dirt path to the sound.

"I've been waiting for you both. What has taken you so long? We must be quick. Come in." Relic Quinn ushered them through the door, peering in the darkness, then slammed the door shut.

Dante surveyed the room, beholding the large leather-bound spell books on the shelf in the corner and spices, mixing bowls, and glass jars on a table.

"Proper Crypt, you may sit on this sofa as we discuss important matters." Relic Quinn gestured toward the large green sofa on the other end of the room. He ushered Relic Caligari into a side room. "Would you like any tea while you wait?" he added, almost as an afterthought.

Dante shook his head. "No, thank you." He sat on the sofa and waited.

It wasn't unusual to be excluded in conversations among Relics. As a Proper, Dante was a full-fledged warlock but only by one year. It took centuries to become a Relic and only a few were ever given that privilege.

Dante sat on the edge of the sofa, straining to hear their conversation. It proved to be futile, for even the faintest sound didn't carry from the room they were in.

He shivered. A smoldering small fireplace in the corner heated the room. He stood and added a log then warmed his hands over the fire.

Before long, voices rose, and a crash came from behind the door, startling Dante.

"Absolutely not! I forbid it."

"Get over yourself, Relic Quinn. You aren't the sole deciding factor here. It would be foolish if we didn't find out."

"If that's how you feel, then get out! Take it with you. I never want to see it again."

Relic Caligari and Relic Quinn emerged from the room. Relic Quinn's face was beet red, and his eyes bulged.

Relic Caligari's demeanor was calm, except for the mild twitching of his left eyebrow—an imperceptible reaction to most. "Proper Crypt, we're leaving." Relic Caligari waved toward the door.

Dante stood, following him through the doorway.

Relic Quinn huffed and slammed the door just as they exited.

"Uh ... I'm confused. We came here for his help, not to be thrown out," Dante said.

"We have procured what we came for, even without a cordial exit. Now come along, we must not dawdle. Our journey awaits."

Dante was left standing at the doorstep, mouth agape in utter confusion.

RELIC CALIGARI CLUTCHED A FOREIGN MAP.

Dante peered over his shoulders numerous times, attempting to recognize the landscape. He could no longer bear the curiosity. "Relic Caligari, where does that map depict? I do not recognize the borders as part of Arish."

"My young Proper Crypt, you have many things yet to learn. Our world of Arish is not the only world. In fact there are many worlds, some we know about and others we do not." He outstretched his hand so Dante could get a better view. "This is a map of a new world we know little about. We have a name and a few stories about it. Come, we are to investigate this new place."

Relic Caligari and Dante stopped walking once they

came to a large open field. They grabbed their crystals, squeezed tight and concentrated on the map of the new world.

A loud whooshing sound was followed by a loud buzz in Dante's ears. His vision became clear, and he knew he was no longer in Arish.

They stood in a narrow walkway surrounded by strange looking red-hue stones. The ground was made of stones, and noises came from outside the walkway. Dante followed Relic Caligari into the clearing where they saw contraptions transporting people.

"What are *those*?" Dante asked.

"I do not know. They are strange aren't they?" He peered into the opening. "Come, we must find a place to rest. We can devise a plan then find what we're looking for."

"What are we looking for, Relic Caligari?"

"Ari people."

Dante's eyes rounded and his jaw slackened. *What would my people be doing here?*

RELIC CALIGARI and Dante sat around the fireplace, warming their hands and feet. The furniture seemed close to the furniture in Arish; however, the materials were different, and the patterns were strange.

Dante clutched his crystal, uncertainty written on his face. He fidgeted with his crystal and startled at every sound. "I don't understand. Where did this map come from?"

Relic Caligari shifted in his seat. "You know the Augur sees many things and records them for us."

Dante nodded.

"A few months ago, the Augur had one of his visions, and the result was this map." Relic Caligari proffered the map toward Dante. "The other Relics decided it should go into Archives until it was explored and deemed safe."

"So then why is it out, and why are we looking for Ari people?"

"It was released before it should have been. Some Ari people found the map and decided to explore it. Our people have been coming to this land for months."

"How was it released? Shouldn't it have been protected from the Propers?"

"It *should* have been, yes, but alas, that is still being explored."

"So is this land safe?"

"We're still unsure, but we must know before this gets out of hand."

Dante nodded. New lands were worrisome. Would they have magic as Arish did? Would they understand magic and the Ari way?

"What can we do? What must we look for?"

"I know where a few Ari people are staying. They have remained close to the initial drop off from the map. Past where they are staying, I'm unsure of much else."

"Hmm ... when do we begin?"

"Now, if you're ready."

"Okay. Where are we going?"

"A few streets over. I can sense the magic is concentrated in that area."

Dante stood, followed by Relic Caligari. Dante waited as Relic Caligari stretched and headed to the front door. He opened the door, letting a waft of chilly air sweep through the room.

In the short time they had been sitting by the fire, things had changed. People wore face coverings and had scary-looking features. Red hues dripped from their faces and on their attire. *Blood.*

Dante stopped walking. "What is happening here? Has there been a war since we were in that building?"

Relic Caligari shook his head. "I'm unsure. It seems to be a ritual of some kind. All I see are these strange features."

Relic Caligari stopped someone walking near them. "Excuse me. May I ask you a question?"

The scary image nodded.

"What is on your face?"

A hand reached up and removed it. "This?" The object was gestured toward Dante and Relic Caligari. "A mask. It's my costume for Halloween. Isn't it the berries?"

"What's Halloween?" Dante asked.

Without the *mask*, the mysterious person was a man. "Halloween? Aren't you two dressed up?"

Relic Caligari and Dante looked at their robes then back to the man. "It's October thirty-first, you know? We dress up and celebrate Halloween. It's the bees knees." The man moved closer to Relic Caligari and Dante. "The twenty-first building has some giggle water, if you know what I mean. It's the place to be tonight!" The man waved, put on his mask and walked away.

Dante surveyed the area. More people seemed to be in costumes, like the man had described. Dante rubbed his chin. "Relic Caligari, I don't understand anything that man said. Do you?"

"Not entirely, but let's head to the twenty-first building. I think we'll find some insight there."

Dante nodded, and they meandered, looking for the twenty-first building.

THE TWENTY-FIRST BUILDING turned out to be another stone building with a red hue. The building materials were strange to Dante, but they seemed to cover the area. The outside was barren for a place that was supposed to be busy.

"Relic Caligari, I don't understand. That man said this was the place to be tonight. It looks vacant."

"Ah, things are not always what they seem." Relic Caligari grabbed his crystal and concentrated.

"What is it?"

"I can feel magic concentrated in this area. This building does contain a few Ari people. We must find a way in."

A group of people wearing the same *masks* walked by and turned down the corner.

Relic Caligari eyed them warily and followed. He waved Dante toward him as he crept around the corner.

The group paused at a side door and whispered something toward the door. It opened then quickly shut.

Relic Caligari faced Dante. "That must be how we get in."

"But what did they say?"

"I'm not sure. But stay close."

Dante nodded.

They approached the door and knocked.

"Password," a gruff voice said.

Dante looked at Relic Caligari, and raised his hands and whispered, "What do we do?"

Relic Caligari grabbed his crystal and concentrated. "Tell me the password."

"Ford," the gruff voice choked out.

Dante looked toward Relic Caligari who shrugged.

A cough came from behind the door. "Password. I don't have all day."

"Ford," Relic Caligari repeated.

The door swung open. The gruff voice belonged to a gray-haired man of tall and muscular stature. He led them both down a long dark passageway that opened into a large room with high ceilings. Tables were stationed around the rooms and a high top by the side. Centered in the middle of the room was a large floor set high above the regular floor.

"What is this place?" Dante asked.

"I'm unsure. Let's split up. If you find Ari people, merely hold your crystal and focus. I'll find you."

Dante nodded.

Relic Caligari took the stairs to an upper platform as Dante mingled around the tables. People were dressed in masks and weird attire. Small colorful things were attached to the end of skirts, and women were swishing them around as they moved.

Dante surveyed the room. These people dressed differently, and, with the masks, it was difficult to tell who, if anyone, was from Arish. Dante sat at a table and watched. He would have to blend in if he didn't want anyone to cause attention. He might not know this place, but he knew well enough that outsiders were not usually welcomed.

Dante noticed the men wore pants and the gruesome masks, while the women had those swishing small objects going around them. This *Halloween* was strange. Who wanted to hide their faces from others, especially in such a cruel way?

A group of women appeared on the higher platform. They had even stranger costumes—more things to swish around. Dante stood and got closer to them. Before he was too close, they erupted into song. The tune was strange.

Music was used differently in Arish. It was for ritual. It

was only done at certain times, like at the Rite of the Callows. *Which I'm missing—the first once since my own Rite.* It was strange that this world's so-called Halloween fell on a sacred Rite for the Arish people. Could they be connected? Dante shook his head. *Impossible.* This world was only recently found. How could that be so?

Dancing with unfamiliar movements accompanied the song. It was obvious they were dancing, but Dante hadn't learned this movement from his studies as a Callow. It was mandatory to learn of other cultures and worldly traditions before one became a Proper—a full-fledged warlock.

Dante drew his attention from the performance. He needed to find Ari people, and he needed to find them fast. The longer they were in this world, the stranger it seemed.

Dante's crystal pulsated with energy. Relic Caligari must be calling him; maybe he found some of their people. Dante searched the crowd and held the crystal. As he got closer, it pulsated harder, until he turned the corner and almost ran into Relic Caligari and two of their people—a man and a woman older than Dante.

"Ah, Proper Crypt, thank you for joining us," Relic Caligari said.

Dante nodded.

Relic Caligari turned toward the other two Propers. "Proper Delacroix and Proper Dupree. We must speak with you at once."

Delacroix? As in Isadora Delacroix? How did she end up in this new world? She was an amazing witch from Arish. If he was correct, they had their Rite of the Callows at least five years ago, making them twenty-six.

The Propers exchanged glances then gestured toward a backroom. Dante and Relic Caligari followed them. Dante peered around the corner—set on edge. Where were these Ari people taking them?

Proper Dupree propped the door open. "Come in and sit. It will be easier to hear each other in here."

Relic Caligari nodded and walked through the doorway first. Dante was the last to enter. The other Propers were still required to show reverence to Relic Caligari, but Dante was no one to them.

Relic Caligari sat in the corner, facing everyone else. He laid his hands on his lap and smiled a gentle smile. Dante had seen that expression before; Relic Caligari was trying to put their guests at ease, but he could only imagine the ferocity that would appear if these two weren't forthcoming with information.

"Ah. I'm glad we found you two. We've been on quite the journey today." He leaned closer to the two Propers. "I could ask how you *two* arrived here as well, but I'll save that question for later. The more important question I wish to ask first is what have you learned of this place?"

Proper Dupree spoke first. "We're in a place called South Carolina. They have states instead of provinces, and they're governed differently, but also similarly."

"And what of the people?" Relic Caligari asked.

"They seem to be similar to Ari people …"

"But?"

"No magic," Proper Delacroix said.

Relic Caligari touched his face and squinted his brows. "Ah, I see."

Dante watched Proper Delacroix as she sat next to Proper Dupree. They seemed connected but weren't touching. Something was happening between them, but Dante couldn't deduce what it was.

"Why haven't you both returned home?" Relic Caligari asked.

"It's complicated," Proper Dupree said.

Proper Delacroix's cheeks reddened, and she averted her eyes.

Something is definitely going on with them.

"Well, do explain," Relic Caligari said.

Proper Dupree looked from Proper Isadora to Relic Caligari and back again.

What was happening? Isadora Delacroix was not just some ordinary witch. She was instrumental in creating several spells that had helped the Arish people during the famines the previous few years. She had helped restore the soil and ushered us forward in thinking. Why would she leave Arish to be in this place called *South Carolina*?

"Well ...?"

"It's my fault, Relic Caligari," Proper Delacroix said.

Relic Caligari's eyebrows rose. "You?"

She nodded. "I've fallen in love with a man from this world."

Dante gasped.

Relic Caligari's eyes widened ever so slightly then relaxed. "In love?"

She nodded. "And that's not all."

"Oh?"

"He loves me as well and has proposed."

"Proposed?"

She waved her left hand with a glistening rock on it. "Yes. That's what they call our fusion rituals. But of course, a little different with no magic."

"And you accepted this?"

She nodded. "And when I did, things changed ..."

Relic Caligari was very still and silent.

"Changed how?" Dante asked.

"My ... well, my magic has diminished."

Relic Caligari stood. "Diminished? But you're one of

the great witches of your generation. Are you to tell me you've lost your magic?"

Proper Delacroix took the crystal from her pocket and passed it to Relic Caligari. Her crystal was a brilliant blue —the color of sapphires.

As he turned it around in his fingers, he closed his eyes. The crystal turned over and over again. He opened his eyes and returned it to Proper Delacroix. "I see. I do feel the magic has been drained from you. Your crystal struggles to concentrate what is left." He stroked his chin. "And you said this happened when you accepted this man?"

She nodded.

Proper Dupree stood and approached Relic Caligari. "Is there something we can do? I won't leave without her."

How could Proper Dupree have let one of the best witches of the time fall in love with *these* people? He should have been watching her carefully.

Relic Caligari patted the man's shoulder. "I'm afraid this is unprecedented in our history. We've come across many worlds without magic, but we've never heard of a witch, especially one of her magnitude, losing her magic. We've also never had our people stay in another world with no magic and fuse their souls."

"So, there's no hope?"

"I do not wish to give hope when I'm unsure. I'll have to council with the other Relics about this. But she may very well be without magic for the rest of her life."

Proper Delacroix crossed her arms. "I am not leaving, Hunter. I love him. You can go back to Arish. I'm fine here."

Proper Dupree scowled.

Relic Caligari approached Dante. "Let's talk in the

hallway." He eyed Proper Dupree and Proper Delacroix. "We'll be back. I suggest you work things out."

Relic Caligari and Dante returned to the hallway and stopped on the other side of the doorway.

Dante leaned against the door and listened.

"Hunter, why did you say that? You know how I feel about Robert. He completes me. You'll never understand what that feels like."

"Isadora … we came here to discover a new world, to learn of their practices and take it back home. That was the mission. We've done it before. You've cured famine and lead us into a new age from the worlds we've discovered. You just want to give that all up?"

"Hunter, stop. I'm done listening to this. We were fellow Callows and now fellow Propers, but I owe you nor them anything. I deserve to marry whom I love."

Relic Caligari moved Dante away from the door and grasped his crystal. He whispered a short chant then looked at Dante. "I do not wish for them to hear us." He stroked his chin in fervor. "I'm displeased with these events. An Ari person falling in *love* with one of these people? What will the rest of our world say when they find out? And, to top it off, she is *losing* her magic." He shook his head and paced. "No, this simply cannot do. We can't risk losing our heritage and magic to these people. We must force them back and tell the other Relics."

Could it be true? Could she have gotten her new spells from other worlds? Were the Relics really worried about this place or her secret being revealed? Dante didn't enjoy strong arming anyone, but sometimes, what one likes and what one must don't work together. Relic Caligari had been most serious when he had said they would be forced back.

They reentered the room and surprised both Proper

Dupree and Proper Delacroix with a sleeping spell until they could safely return them to Arish. They dragged them from the building and to their original location where they had arrived. To prevent any outsiders learning what was happening, they used magic to conceal them all.

They used their maps of Arish and thought intently on the center of their world. It would be the location of the Rite of the Callows, and it would be just in time. Dante held up Proper Dupree, and Relic Caligari held up Proper Delacroix. Relic Caligari was in the middle of a heated debate with the other Relics.

"You can't be serious, Relic Caligari. Those accusations are absurd!" Relic Bask shouted.

"You've interrupted one of our most sacred rituals!" another Relic yelled.

Relic Caligari raised both hands in protest. "What I have to say is of grave importance. What I've learned about the new world is devastating and must be dealt with."

The other Relics quieted momentarily, so he continued. "I found these two Propers on the other side. They appear to have been in that place for quite some time. This world is with no magic, and the people seem to be similar to us physically. But Proper Delacroix has made a grave mistake." He leaned in for the Relics to hear. "She has *no* magic."

The Relics gasped.

"No magic? Why that is absurd. We can't lose our magic," Relic Bask said.

"Apparently, we can." Relic Caligari awoke Proper Delacroix in an instant. He shoved her toward the other Relics. "Tell them of your story."

Proper Delacroix's face reddened and she wobbled. "I … uh." She cleared her throat. "I arrived in this new world several months ago. I went with my friend, Proper Dupree. We hoped for an exciting journey." She peered at all the faces staring at her. "Which we found and more. I fell in love with a man from this world, and he proposed."

The other Relics scrunched their faces, just like Relic Caligari had done.

"It is their version of Fusion of Souls. They get married in their world with a ceremony. I accepted ... then my magic vanished."

"Vanished? All at once?"

She shook her head. "Not all at once, but I could instantly tell there was a difference. Within a week, it was gone, and I could no longer concentrate it through my crystal."

The Relics gasped then shouted to each other.

"This is an outrage!"

"Despicable!"

"What a waste!"

Dante shifted Proper Dupree in his arms. This whole story was absurd to him. How could she have lost her magic? A witch unlike any other. Her abilities had come quickly, naturally, and without much effort. For some witches and warlocks, it took years to master their natural abilities as Callows. For others, like Proper Delacroix, it was instant. As a Callow, she possessed more control than some Propers ever managed. When she had gone through her Rite, she improved vastly.

Relic Caligari raised both arms to hush them. "Relics, please. We must focus on what is to be done. We only found those two Propers in this new world. We know more are missing. We must take a stand."

Relic Bask, the leader of the Relics, had been silent during this retelling. He rose and everyone stared at him.

"We must do the only thing we can do. We must stop it from happening in the future."

"But how?" Relic Caligari asked.

"Scribe!" Relic Bask shouted. "Write this down for all."

A scribe scrambled from the crowd awaiting the Rite of the Callows. Other Propers stared intently at the Relics. The Ari people were abuzz with hushed tones.

"Yes, Relic Bask?" the scribe asked.

"Are you ready?"

He nodded.

"From henceforth, Ari people will be betrothed to someone else from the Ari community on the Rite of the Callows decided by the Relics. We will never again have someone *marry* these Souls."

"Souls?" the scribe asked.

Relic Bask nodded. "Souls is the name I give these magic-less people. And our people shall not marry them. To keep our heritage and ways safe, we must stick to each other. If these people can persuade a Proper with as much ability as Proper Delacroix and lose their magic, anyone else could as well. We can't risk it."

Relic Bask turned his attention to Proper Delacroix. "You will be punished. You have lost your sacred ability by loving this Soul. You'll be permitted to live in this new world ... but *alone*. We'll be watching you, and, if you disobey us, you'll be punished more severely for your crimes."

Proper Delacroix threw herself at Relic Bask's feet. "Please, no. I beg you to reconsider."

"I will not. You have chosen this life for yourself—one without magic and against our people. You will deal with those consequences."

Relic Bask nudged Proper Dupree awake. As he stirred, Relic Bask helped him stand. Proper Dupree swayed back and forth. Dante stood near him and kept him from toppling over.

"You're just as much to blame for this treachery. As such, your punishment will be to live in constant watch over Proper Delacroix. You'll see that she does not marry this Soul and stays alone. You'll be granted with extended life to watch her, until her dying breath. Then you too will die. You may not marry or do anything else but watch her. Do you understand?"

Proper Dupree blinked several times and nodded.

"So be it." He faced Relic Caligari. "Disperse of them would you?"

Relic Caligari nodded.

"Grab them and lead them ahead," Relic Caligari directed Dante in hushed tones.

Dante did as he was told. He would not risk angering the Relics any further. How would the Ari people take this new decree? No longer could they choose who they should fuse their souls to. While Dante understood they deserved punishment, he did not understand why everyone else should as well. Strange times were ahead, and he was unsure of what it all would mean.

Catacombs

Andrew Parker

They were just kids. Kids doing what kids did. A dare, no doubt. Two boys, two girls. They'd found the old entrance in the woods and had dropped down into the upper tunnel. Drenched by the downpour outside, they paused to shake their coats off. Great beads of water flew in all directions. Umbrellas were shaken and closed. Two more lanterns lit. The rumble of thunder found its way into the musty tunnel.

Bones, named for obvious reasons, was the first skeleton they came upon. He laid in his hollow in the wall, in his eternal rest. Clothing long gone to dust. Flesh wasted away. A few dried ligaments were all that was left holding him together.

Bones loved to feign the darkest depression for the newest corpses. When they asked him what was wrong, he'd respond, while shaking his disconnected left pinky, "I don't know. I'm just falling apart."

He'd then howl with laughter—as much as the dead could at least, and revel in the corpses's hock and despair in the face of his humor. At least in those who had enough flesh left to show shock and despair.

The kids looked at Bones.

"Touch it," one of the girls said.

"You touch it," a boy responded.

"What's in it if I do?" the other boy asked.

"I'll let you do what I told you the other night you couldn't," the other girl said.

"What did you tell——" the first girl started.

"Never mind. Are you going to or not?" the second girl asked the boy.

Apparently, whatever it was that he had hoped to do, that she'd denied him the doing of, was motivation enough for the boy. He reached out and touched one of Bones's ribs.

Nothing happened, of course. He roughly pushed the rib cage, shaking Bones in the process.

"Boo," said Bones.

Of course, it wasn't really "Boo." Given the complete lack of vocal cords, a tongue, lips, and other necessary soft tissues, it was more of a rattly moan. Bones could only make noise with his—well, with his bones.

They all shrieked, and I believed the boys shrieked both louder and with a higher pitch than the girls. I wondered if they had been in a boys' choir before adolescence had come to destroy their happiness. I hoped they had.

One of the boys brought his umbrella up like a great long sword and brought it down on Bones's leg. There was a loud crack as the bone snapped in two.

Now as you can probably imagine, being dead and hanging out in a catacomb can be terribly boring. While Bones, bless his soul, did bring some regular comic relief, we just didn't get much variety.

The kids took off down the tunnel, screaming like banshees. That they headed the wrong way, towards the depths, rather than the entrance, only added to our amusement. The hundreds of us that were aware found ourselves unable to contain our glee. A symphony of creaking, rattling, wheezing, and moaning ensued. The echoes of our own decomposition twisted laughter mixed with the echoes of the kids' shrieks. It sounded like a large group of musicians who didn't know how to play their instruments. Our laughter inspired an even higher level of terror in the kids with a commensurate increase in pitch and volume of the shrieking.

Body memories took over, and we all started to shake, as we had when we'd laughed whence still living. One poor soul, who'd been dead only a couple of weeks, shook the rest of her remaining soft stuff right off, leaving smooth, slippery, white bone.

I was aware of Hangman in his hollow in the wall across from me. Hangman had been a hangman. Then his fondness for hanging people that hadn't any reason to be hung was discovered. He was then hung by another hangman. He was little more than a loose pile of bones, but the body memory for laughter remained true, and he rattled in his little pile with mirth. Like an enamel coated jumping bean, a tooth hopped its way off the pile. It vibrated and jumped across the hollow in the wall and off onto the tunnel floor, landing with a *click*.

The kids skidded to a stop when they came to a dead end. They all bent over, gasping. One of them wheezed, a high-pitched whistle with each exhale. They stood there for some minutes, catching their breaths. Stark terror calming to mild panic.

A skeletal hand laid in the tunnel center. It shook, indicating that at least part of the original owner, Edward, was enjoying the entertainment. It started clawing itself toward them.

This prompted a new round of shrieking. The boys still out classed their feminine counterparts in volume and pitch, though the girls were catching up. A high-pitched whistle rode the cadence as the wheezer ran. They sprinted past a hollow with a relatively new resident, the odor of decay leaving them retching between gasps.

As was the case with the living, even the dead ran out of laughing steam after a while. The kids eventually found their way back to the right tunnel and escaped to the surface. It was doubtless that we would be the men and women of their nightmares for weeks to come.

It was all good fun, and we remembered with fondness, days in the living times, when one's stomach would ache, and one would silently shake with tears streaming down fat cheeks, because something was truly hilarious beyond sounds. But alas, I digress.

There'd be hell to pay. It was just a matter of when it would come to collect.

The next morning, a few of us gathered in the large mausoleum. A great dome, its lower quarter was below ground, level with the upper tunnels.

Bones came around the bend of the tunnel. Stump tap-tapping against the wall. A steady percussion, as if to a cheerful tune. He held his broken lower leg in his hand and rattled it like a maraca as he hopped on the remaining intact leg. Bones was truly the most jovial dead person I'd ever met.

Bones entered the mausoleum. He had stuck his disconnected pinky in his nose hole. The tapered point hung, hooked, out in front of his face, giving an impression of a beak.

We were bleak, having spent the night remembering

laughter and images of joys of the flesh from the living years. A contrast to our current eternal denial of them.

Occasionally, a new corpse would come in, still fleshed. Someone would have and share a vivid memory of passionate days from living times. Then we all found memories of satin skin, firm muscles, hot breath, and tender kisses floating to the tops of our minds. Lovely lilies breaking through the otherwise normal scum of our thoughts. Days of melancholy always followed. It was the same if someone shared a memory of food or drink or even getting slapped or run over by a carriage.

We always hated whomever shared the initial thought, for triggering our own. The hate only lasted a few days, as we needed each other and ostracization was a really a horror of the living, not of the dead.

Bones's entrance brought the previous night's escapades to the surface again. Lower jaws cracked as corpses approximated smiles.

"Well, that was a good one," Bones said.

There was a universal assent.

"That might have been the one, Bones," I replied.

I was accepted as a leader. I'd been there a long time, but I didn't have the degree of decomposition of most. I'd been murdered by a man angry at my liberties with his eldest daughter. He'd buried me in a bog. I'd been there a month or so before a farmer's dog found me. I was then interred in the catacombs.

During my short duration in the bog, my corpse had absorbed enough tannin to preserve most of my tissues, but not so much as to render me hard.

Bones shrugged, bouncing his shoulders up and down. Scapulae made a scraping sound as they rubbed the back of his rib cage.

"What's he going to do? Kill me?" Bones asked.

We didn't talk with voices of course. None of us had them. We could converse by virtue of thought-talking.

"No, worse. He could take your essence to the depths with him."

"Well then, to you, my pickled friend, I shall bequeath my newest instrument, so that when death has you rattled, you can rattle back at it," he said. He shook the foot, and toe bones rattled against each other.

There was the equivalent of a thought giggle. Bones turned to another.

"And to you, Captain, I leave my prized pinky," he said, plucking the pinky bone out of his nose hole and pointing it at the shabby corpse next to me.

Captain had been a sea captain at one time, or so he said. The uniform, tattered as it now was, indicated his claim was probably true. He'd sailed the seven seas on her majesty's ships. He'd retired with wealth he'd obtained on the side, while in her majesty's service. The first day land-bound, he took a small skiff out to fish. A storm came up, and he drowned. It was an embarrassment to him. Commanding vessels over the great deep for decades, only to drown in a fishing pond.

There was a hiss coming from above and below. From in front, behind, and from the sides. As if there was any light in the mausoleum to be dimmed, it grew darker. Not the darkening of visible light. It was the darkening of hope and happiness. He was coming.

There was only one cardinal rule in the hereafter. Never let the living know we were conscious, much less mobile. The risk was that they would make the connection between our essence and our deceased bodies. That they'd go to extreme measures to destroy the dead so that the essence couldn't remain.

Even with Hangman and others of his advanced

decomposition, the essence still stayed. If the living took to cremating or cutting the dead into pieces and then scattering them over great distances, what would happen to the essences? Remaining attached to all the parts, the essence could be stretched, the consciousness spread thin enough that it could no longer work as a cohesive thing. The sense of self, the identity's existence, could be extinguished.

He was simply protecting the dead. Both those currently dead and all the living, whose turns would inevitably come.

We were talking, waiting, and all of a sudden, he was there. The Prince of Darkness. We didn't know if he had a corpse. He certainly didn't keep it with him as he traveled, if he did. He was the anomaly, the one that could travel far and wide away from his corpse. Or did he even have one? Had he even ever been alive?

He was like a dark mist or fog, coalesced into a form that varied between cloud, human, and some things that could still tickle the deepest primal fears of even the dead. At times his face would take form, when he wanted the impact of 'eye-to-eye' contact.

I bowed my head. Others did the same as he scanned our boney faces. His gaze rested on Bones a second. Bones raised the disconnected foot and waved with it.

There was a thought, like a high pitch. Someone had started to laugh and choked it off.

"What happened?" the prince asked, his voice calm.

"I did it," Bones said.

"I know you did it. What happened?"

He looked at me, waiting.

I projected my memory of the event to him. A memory that was both mine and the views of others that had witnessed it. He experienced it as if he had been there.

There was no discernable response. He stood silent, waiting.

Corpses could get fidgety. Boney feet shuffled on granite floor. Someone drummed the cover of the marble coffin. Click-ity-click-ity-clack, click-ity-click-ity-clack, the thumb making a different sound than the fingers.

"Edward," the prince said.

The independent hand, the one that had frightened the kids in the tunnel, came around the corner of the coffin stand and finger crawled toward the dark presence.

"Why did you intentionally frighten them?" the prince asked.

"I was caught up in the moment, master."

"I am not your or anyone's master. I am the guardian of the dead."

While the dead did debate and argue, disagreements were seldom over semantics. If he wasn't our master, then there was no such thing. Bones, distracted with his detached appendages, snapped to attention with the prince's statement. He was willing to debate the term. I warned Bones off, thrusting my face forward at him. A dead man's version of a glare. Miraculously, Bones refrained. There might be hope for him yet.

"Yes, mas ... es," Edward said.

"Edward, you are to go back to the tunnel end where you reside. Dig back down to where the rest of you is buried in the floor. Pull the dirt over yourself and remain there for 50 years."

It was a severe sentence. It was boring enough to be dead, much less relegated to one spot, under the dirt.

"Yes, my prince," Edward said. He pulled himself around and started finger crawling towards the exit tunnel. I'd never seen a hand look dejected before.

"Bones, put yourself in your hollow. Your essence will accompany me to the depths."

I shuddered. The depths. We didn't know what it meant as far as location was concerned. The thought of it led to the depths of despair. We knew it was populated by the essences, the souls of those who'd gone rogue on the prince's single restriction. Mostly those who wouldn't let the living go. Or those who had issues with the living they felt compelled to still resolve. Countless souls from around the world and across time who were the precipitators of ideas such as zombies and vampires, until the Dark Prince got them.

So far as we knew, no one could resist the prince. He had the power to capture and imprison the essence of any of the dead. Bones was nonchalant.

"If there'd been any damage, we'd know by now. How many give credence to the rantings of youth?" Bones remarked.

"You have a trend," the prince said.

"Trend?"

"Seventeen years ago. The diggers making new hollows in the walls. You moved your arm."

"They were making a disturbance. It must've vibrated, making my arm settle."

"Eight times?"

"If I recall, it was a significant disturbance," Bones retorted.

"It must've been indeed, given the arm moved back and forth, off the hollow edge and back on again, across your ribs and back flat once more," the Dark Prince said.

"Well, yes. There may have been seismic activity."

"Given the lack of any such activity in this area for millennia ..."

"Well, perhaps, Your Darkness, I've had a couple of

lapses of judgment. Two incidents hardly constitute a trend."

The prince dealt with the dead's' penchant for calling him a prince, referring to him as a darkness, master, etc., with pained tolerance. He'd shared his name in eons past. Even in thought-speak, it was beyond what any of us could pronounce. The darkness reference was inevitable. His form vacillated between black and the darkest indigo. We mused that indigo was when he was happy. None of us shared the theory with him.

"Seventy-three years ago, you turned your head and clacked your jaw at member of a burial entourage," he said.

"My ligaments must've been settling. Relaxing."

"A pattern of relaxing, constricting, relaxing, and constricting, rapidly in succession?"

"You seem to be perseverating on patterns and trends, Your Darkness."

Did the Dark Prince just sigh?

"'Your Darkness' is not an accurate title for me," the prince said, his color turning the deepest black.

We didn't know what it meant when he turned so black, but given circumstances, it couldn't be good. Bones was testing his patience.

Bones noticed the wonderful timing between the prince's statement and the increased depth of blackness. He held his hands out to clarify. "Well, obviously—"

"Bones," I interrupted. He stopped his folly.

"My apologies, Your Dar—My apologies. What if I can prove there was no harm done?" Bones asked.

"Prove?" the prince asked.

"Yeah. If there was no harm …"

The prince considered it. "I will be back for your

essence tomorrow. If you can convince me there was no harm, I will allow you to stay."

There was a loud snap in the air as the prince disappeared. It was as if an oppressive weight had been lifted.

"Prove?" I asked.

Bones shrugged with the scraping of the scapulae. "It was a stall tactic."

"Bones, what are you going to do?"

"You can't resist the Dark Prince. No one can," the Captain said.

"Hey, I've been chilling here for a couple hundred years. I hear it's quite toasty where he keeps his imprisoned souls. Might be a nice chance to warm up," Bones said, carefree as ever.

It was a long day. They all were. We made up and told a lot of stories for lack of new experiences to share. Today, though, all we talked about were Bones and the Dark Prince.

It wasn't just that Bones was our only real comic relief. We liked him. To have him relegated as one of the prince's caged pets was depressing.

Being one of the few older, mobile ones, I wandered the tunnels. Commiserating, talking, strategizing. All we came up with was a mass appeal to the Dark Prince. But appeal to what? His empathy? His compassion? I was not optimistic.

I leaned against the wall by Bones's hollow. He was in his usual reclined position, legs crossed above the break, hands clasped under his skull.

"Well, I can't think of anything," I said.

"I hear you've called an assembly on my behalf tomorrow," Bones replied.

"Yes, we're going to appeal to the Dark Prince."

"Appreciate it. A lot of us could use some assembly." He rattled his detached foot.

"Re-assembly, you mean?" I asked with a smile.

I was one of the very few that could actually pull off a smile. The others who could, soon wouldn't be able to, due to their rates of decomposition.

"I really was serious about leaving you my foot," he said.

"Aren't you worried?"

"Nah. Nothin' I can do. How's worrying going to help?"

"I'd be worried. The depths, Bones. It's the depths."

"Think of all the souls who've never heard my jokes. I'll be a hero."

There was a creak up the tunnel. The entrance gate was moving.

"Best be scarce, friend," Bones said.

I moved down the tunnel into where it would be shadowed, should someone enter with a light. Whispers snuck down the tunnel. Timid footsteps shuffling on the stone steps grew louder.

The next morning, we had as many as possible gathered in the mausoleum. Myself and a couple of fresh deliveries from the other end of the catacombs carried pieces of those that were no longer mobile; allowing their essences to participate.

Bones, always the center of social activity, was singing a funny ballad. Others were engaged in conversation. The air was thick with excitement, fear, and anticipation.

I watched him, surprised at the depth of my affection for my friend. He was a royal pain at times, and it was impossible for anyone to have a serious conversation with him around. Still, he left us with levity in impossible circumstances.

There was the hiss again. Coming from above and below. From in front, behind, and from the sides. Everyone silenced. There came the darkening of hope and happiness.

Then he was there. He surveyed our presence. It was unlikely he'd had such a reception before. All of us were there.

"Bones," he said. His thought-voice calm and penetrating.

"Bags packed and ready," Bones replied.

"Is your companion ready as well?"

As if it were possible, it became even more silent.

"If need be, I'm ready," I answered.

Bodies turned and skulls swiveled as I approached the prince. One poor slob had the unfortunate luck of timing to have his skull come loose. It fell and hit the floor with a dull thud, rolling forward and stopping at the prince's feet.

"It needs be," he stated.

"Now see here," Bones said. "There's no use in punishing him. I did the damage."

"I thought you said there was no damage," the prince said.

"I don't believe there is."

"Tell me about your leg."

Everyone looked at Bones's broken leg. The broken portion was reattached to the upper part, splinted.

"Well, yes. I thought it might be nice to spend my last day attached to my body, walking normally," Bones said.

"You know, of course, that I can discern any level of deception," the prince said.

"Well … Yeah."

"Then why do you lie?"

"I was hoping your lie detector might be out of order."

"I don't get out of order, Bones."

The Dark Prince was different. Curious? He turned toward me and said, "Show me."

I projected Bones's and my combined experience, so that everyone there would know.

THE FOOTSTEPS STOPPED. More whispering and the strike of a match. A cloud of smoke rose to the ceiling of the tunnel. Two people at the base of the stairs fumbled with a lantern. Having succeeded in lighting it, they continued their shuffle toward us.

As they got closer, we recognized them.

"I'll be damned," Bones said.

"I never would've expected," I added.

It was the two boys from the other night. They approached, hesitant. I was far enough down the hall that with my tannin darkened complexion, they couldn't see me.

One boy leaned toward Bones.

"I … I'm sorry I broke your leg," he said.

The other boy nodded and said, "We di … di … di … didn't know. We didn't know that you were still …"

They looked at each other and then at Bones. From Bones, they looked down the tunnel in my direction.

"We didn't know that all of you were still here," he continued.

"We came to fix your leg, if you like," the first boy said.

Their eyes darted about, and they kept looking down the tunnel, both in my direction and back towards the dark stairs. Perhaps making sure that no one, no thing, snuck up on them. Perhaps also keeping in mind the right direction, should escape become indicated. They had shifting eyes, tense muscles, and shallow breaths. They appeared on the edge of terror.

"Can you let us know if that's okay?"

Bones lifted a finger. The boys gasped.

"Does that mean okay?"

Bones nodded his skull. I started to chastise him and realized it didn't matter. He was already condemned to the depths. What was the Dark Prince going to do? Make him take the trip twice?

One of the boys pulled a bundle out from under a heavy, wool coat. He carefully unwrapped it. He placed two dowels, one along each side of the broken leg.

"Hickory," he said. "It should last a long time."

The other boy aligned the pieces of bone and the dowels. The first boy then unwrapped a damp cloth. It contained a long, thin piece of rawhide. The boy tied it off above the break and painstakingly wrapped it downward. He stretched it, keeping the tension high.

I concluded that he had done this before and speculated that there was a doctor or veterinarian in the home. That, or he worked for one.

When he was finished, he said, "When that dries, it'll be stronger than the original bone."

The other boy added, "It'll dry faster if you heat it over a fire or blow ..." They looked at each other, horrified. Bones's rib cage shook.

"Are you laughing?" one of the boys asked.

Bones nodded.

I felt a compulsion to communicate with them. While I'd never known anyone who'd tried, it was assumed that we couldn't think-talk with the living.

I focused on the boy that had so meticulously wrapped the splint. He seemed like a likely lad. I searched for his thought-voice. Very muted, as if from a great distance away, I could hear it. I let mine carry to him. He looked up and around.

"Don't be afraid," I said, over and over again.

"Did you hear that?" he asked the other boy.

"No. What?"

"Someone's telling me not to be afraid."

"What are you doing?" Bones asked. I ignored him.

"I'm coming to you. I'm dead, so be prepared," I said.

"How?" the boy asked.

"This is how we talk to each other. Tell your friend not to be afraid."

He looked at his friend. "It says not to be afraid. It's coming and won't hurt us."

The other boy appeared as if he'd bolt toward the stairs at any moment.

I walked slowly down the tunnel toward them. Their eyes were wide. Moving skeletons were one thing. At least they knew they could use an umbrella on one of them. I truly was the thing nightmares were made of.

"I'm here to greet you and commend you on your courage."

He shared my words with his friend.

"My friend says thank you for fixing his leg," I added.

He looked at Bones. "You're welcome."

His friend backed against the wall opposite of Bones, but kept his eye on me. I didn't advance further.

"Why don't you let people know that you are ... that you are still here with your bodies?" the boy asked. He spoke out loud, not knowing he didn't have to.

"We are forbidden. The living would destroy us to where we couldn't be any more."

"But the other night ... Now," he said.

"Infractions. My friend and I will be punished."

Bones was attentive, but hadn't been able to connect with the boy's thoughts.

"Punished? What, what kind of punishment can you …? By whom?"

I didn't think a description of the Dark Prince or his involvement would help the boys' nerves.

"There are those we answer to. There are rules. We broke them."

"What will happen to you?"

Bones swiveled his skull back and forth between us. The boys were acclimatizing to the situation.

"Who we are will be disconnected from our bodies, and we will be imprisoned," I said.

"Imprisoned? Where? For how long?"

"Somewhere you don't know. Forever."

His demeanor changed. He stood straighter.

"Well, that seems a bit extreme. There was no harm done," he said.

"Those we answer to, believe there was."

"Why? We didn't tell anyone. Everyone would think we were daft."

"The girls," I replied.

He laughed. The good humor traveled down the tunnel. Echoes laughed back. His friend stared at him, his jaw open.

"We told them we'd put some mushroom powder in their food," he explained.

"They weren't upset?"

"No, they thought it was a great trick." I remained silent, and he continued, "It may be that we've used the mushrooms before."

He hung his head and stuck his hands in his pants pockets. One would expect to get reprimanded by an adult for such behavior. Even if the adult was dead.

"Look, tell these, whomever it is, that there was no

harm done. Nobody knows but us, and we're not stupid enough to tell. Who'd believe us?" he asked.

"You're a good young man," I observed.

He smiled. "Thank you."

"We like you and your friends, but you mustn't come back again."

"Oh, we don't plan too, though you're nicer than a lot of live people."

"What's your name?"

"Edgar. What's yours?"

"I don't remember. It's been too long. Goodbye Edgar, Edgar's friend," I said.

They started to turn to leave. Bones all but yelled his question at me.

"Are you serious, Bones?"

Edgar turned back, having heard my thought-voice. I shook my head.

"My friend here," I looked toward Bones, "wants to know if the girl let you do what she hadn't before."

He was confused at first and then a grin of realization split his face. He told his friend, who laughed aloud.

Edgar looked at Bones and said, "Yeah, she did."

They turned and started toward the stairs. I thought Bones was going to jump up and go after them. I was tempted to do so myself. They stopped at the bottom of the stairs, and he turned back towards us. He raised an eyebrow and winked, then puckered and kissed the air.

Ah ... love's first kiss. Bones and I became lost in reawakened memories of rosebud lips, beautiful eyes, and fingers sliding through silky hair.

. . .

THE MAUSOLEUM WAS QUIET. A few murmurs of "Oh …" and "Ah …" with a few more "kisses," mumbled on the side. Boney fingers touched lipless mouths.

The Dark Prince looked long into my face. The mists thinned and his face became clear.

"You could not have communicated with the boy, had he not been pure. His words are true. No harm done." He looked around at the gathering and asked, "What is this?"

"Family," I answered.

Again, he looked long into my face. Calm. Introspective. The corners of his mouth twitched upward, and he nodded.

"Bones," he said.

Bones approached. No jokes. No false bravado. "Yes, my prince."

"You put your family in jeopardy. Do not interact with the living again."

"Yes, my prince."

"You are pardoned."

"Thank you."

The Dark Prince looked off into the distance. "Edward. You are pardoned of your crime and free to move about again."

He looked at me and drew something out of his … robes? It was a small, luminescent ball. He handed it to me.

"Roll this around the gap of the gate and frame. It will create an unbreakable seal," he said.

"Considerate it done," I replied.

There was a loud snap, and the prince was gone. It was nothing short of riotous. Congratulations for pardons. Congratulations for daring conversations with the living.

"Hey," Bones began. "Did I ever tell you about the man that was buried alive?"

"It was a grave mistake," hundreds of voices answered.

"Oh, you must've heard that one on the living side," Bones said. We walked, and he looked at me. "My jokes are getting old. I'm going to have to get out of here a bit and learn some new ones."

I froze in my tracks and stared at him.

He pointed his finger at me, thumb extended upward, and said, "Heh, heh. Gotchya!"

The Maddening Cry

Gerri R. Gray

E ngland—1647

MATTHEW OPENED his eyes and stared into the thick darkness that surrounded him. His slumber had not been peaceful. Despite being the finest witch-finder in all of England and an executioner both feared and reviled by peasantry and nobility alike, he was a man who always slept quite soundly. His dreams were often made pleasant by the recollected sights and sounds of his victims' final agonies. However, this night was different for him. A horrific nightmare, unlike any his deep and soothing sleep had ever given rise to, now tormented his mind with a scene that struck terror within his righteous heart and swathed his body in a cold rigor.

In a frightful and most peculiar dream, he found himself lying still upon a bed with his arms crossed over his chest in the manner of a corpse. Six women, each attired in sweeping gowns of black crepe, surrounded him. Their hands were ashen in color, and veils of black lace covered their faces. They suddenly erupted in shrieks and loud disconcerting wails that sliced through the inky emptiness of the night like the banshees of Irish folklore presaging a death. Matthew was desirous to silence the congregation of noisemakers, for he found their clamor most maddening and abhorrent to his ears.

He attempted to vocalize his objection to their ungodly cries to no avail. He then heard the sound of footsteps and watched as two burly men approached his bed, their faces leathery and expressionless, and the garments covering their bodies void of any color but black. The women made haste to step away from his bed yet persisted in their dreadful wailing as the men took hold of his body with their gloved hands. Without uttering a word, they lifted it up from the straw mattress and then carried it to a waiting coffin.

Filled with terror, Matthew attempted to free himself from their grips but was alarmed to find that the power to move his arms and legs was foregone. He made an effort to open his mouth and cry out; however, his lips would not part for him despite his best efforts. His entire body was frozen and rigid in a paralytic state from which he was unable to snap out of. The sight and sound of the coffin lid closing above him filled his eyes and ears, and then, in the ensuing darkness, he heard shovelfuls of earth raining down upon the top of the lid, one after another after another, until a deathly silence overtook the noise and the nightmare came to an abrupt and merciful end.

Matthew awoke drenched in a cold perspiration that clung to his clammy flesh like droplets of dew on morning leaves and blades of grass. He inhaled deeply and then sighed with relief. It was simply a bad dream, he reassured himself. Nothing more than a mere figment of his imagination. The thought soon crossed his mind that his nightmare could very well have been the doings of some vengeful witch versed in the evil ways of poppet magic or some other diablerie.

He then let out a hearty laugh, confident that he would sooner or later discover the true identity of this creature and, with the purification of a blazing fire, command her corrupted, devil-fornicating soul to an eternal damnation in the fiery bowels of hell.

He truly believed himself to be a pious man, despite the sadistic pleasure he derived from the brutal acts of torture that he inflicted upon the naked bodies of accused witches and warlocks in order to obtain their confessions. It mattered not if their bleeding lips denounced the devil and swore their allegiance to Almighty God, especially if witnesses had presented spectral evidence against the accused. These minions of Old Scratch, as he liked to call the Prince of Darkness, thought themselves to be clever and well-versed in the ways of trickery.

However, the witch-finder prided himself to be a man immune to satanic subterfuge. With each bloodcurdling scream and with each cry of agonizing pain, his heart would pump with frenzied excitement. And even greater would be his arousal, bringing a delicious tingling to his loins whenever his cruel, but necessary, duties as a servant of God to eradicate the scourge of witches from the land led him to pretty-faced young sorceresses possessing succulent bosoms and buttocks.

Often, he would have his way with them before his tortures disfigured their attributes and rendered them repulsive to the sight, despite his vows of fidelity that were spoken when he took Elspeth Goode, the unsullied daughter of the local blacksmith, as his wife.

Elspeth was a hard-working, God-fearing lass who could be found each Sunday reciting her prayers in Church. A comely young woman of amiable nature, she was fair of face with long tresses of pale-yellow cascading over her milky-white shoulders. Her eyes, green as those of a water sprite, sparkled with innocence. Her cheeks were pink with a childlike quality, and her lips soft like the petals of roses in early summer.

From the moment he first laid eyes upon her, Matthew was determined to have her all to himself. After a brief courtship that lasted for less than half a year, they were wed.

It was during his third year of marriage to the young Elspeth when a rumor that she used charms to bewitch a neighbor's cow began to circulate throughout the small village in which they resided. She was arrested and made to stand trial, shackled and bearing the bruises, welts, and lacerations inflicted upon her flesh by her very own husband in his determination to force a confession from her.

With tears flowing from her once-sparkling eyes, Elspeth pleaded for him to let her live. "Matthew, please! I beg you, spare my life!" she cried out. "I am no more a witch than you are a warlock! For the love of all that is holy, please end this cruelty! I beg you, my husband! Have mercy! I cannot bear this agony much longer!"

In spite of her rounds of torture, which included whippings, the crushing of her thumbs and big toes with a thumbscrew, and the searing of the nipples of her tender, youthful breasts with a red-hot iron poker, Elspeth refused to confess to being a follower of the Old Religion. Her stubborn refusal to admit that she was in league with the devil infuriated Matthew, and no matter how she wept and pleaded for her life, he took no pity upon her.

Not a single tear did Matthew shed on that dismal day in October when he stood with his torch in hand and calmly watched as his battered wife was paraded barefoot through the muddy, dung-filled streets in a manner unfit for either man or beast. She was then dragged, screaming, to a large wooden stake erected in the heart of the village to meet her gruesome fate.

"Burn the witch! Burn the witch!" chanted the villagers, some throwing stones and clods of mud, and all hungering for slaughter. As the cruel chanting of the men, women, and children grew louder and fiercer, an icy wind arose. It howled frightfully through the branches of the trees as if hundreds of witches were careening on their broomsticks through the air around them.

Elspeth was nearly unrecognizable, bearing little resemblance to the eye-pleasing, young maiden the witch-finder had taken as his bride just a few years prior. Her face, once youthful and radiant with zest, was now haggard and abandoned of all hope. Her eyes were swollen shut, given her the appearance of a pummeled boxer. Her nose was broken, her lips cracked and blistered, her hair matted with sweat and dried blood. Her mouth fell open to reveal a number of chipped and bloodstained teeth. Some were missing altogether, having been pulled out by tongs in the torture chamber. Her torso and all of its appendages bore the lacerations and burn marks inflicted upon her by her once-loving spouse.

After she had been securely strapped to the stake with heavy ropes that bit into her wrists and ankles, drawing blood, Matthew tossed his torch at her, setting ablaze the straw and branches and logs that had been piled around the base of the stake. Elspeth's screams, along with the wild cheering of the bloodthirsty mob that had gathered to watch, could be heard throughout the countryside as the hungry flames of the bonfire engulfed her twitching body and her flesh sizzled and burned. The crisp morning air was soon fouled with a putrid-smelling black smoke.

"Blasphemous heathen witch," Matthew grumbled out loud to himself, his words almost taking on the tone of a hissing snake.

Elspeth's execution solidified Matthew's reputation as a virtuous servant unto the Lord. It also sent a clear message that no disciple of the devil would ever be spared the cleansing fire of God's wrath so long as he worked under the esteemed title of "witch-finder general." And that included any witch brazen enough to cast her wicked glamours over him.

As he watched the charred remains of his wife crumble and fall into the glowing embers, he made the sign of the cross and spewed out, "May God have mercy upon her wicked soul." He applauded himself for keeping a solemn face despite the urge of his mouth to rise into a wide smile.

With their bloodlust satisfied, at least for the time being, the crowd began to disperse. Within minutes, the village square was desolate and quiet, save for the occasional pops and crackling sounds emanating from the dying embers.

With his own bloodlust satiated, Matthew turned and made his way down the muddy streets of the village, stopping at a tavern to indulge in shepherd's pie and ale before returning home. He was quite pleased with himself for dispatching yet another witch in strict accordance with God's laws. As he ate his meal and downed his ale with gusto, he reflected on his career as a witch-finder. He had executed so many people, mostly women, he was no longer able to keep count, but it was fair to say that the numbers were in the hundreds. He knew, however, that the job with which he had been tasked was far from being over. Witches were everywhere, initiating new members into Satan's secret sect, holding Black Masses, and defying the Christian faith. It was his duty to rid England of the scourge of sorcery, he told himself.

No sooner had he left the tavern, his belly content with food and drink, did he get struck on the small of his back by a rotting corn cob hurled at him by a ragged urchin girl. He stopped and turned his angry gaze upon the dirty-faced child and shook his fist. "Filthy little she-devil!" he bellowed, as the frightened girl took flight down the muddy street. "Be gone with you before a charge of witchcraft is leveled against you!"

Throughout the years following his wife's horrific execution, Matthew gave little thought to her as he continued his righteous reign of terror. He had simply done what needed to be done and felt not the slightest amount of remorse. Immersed in his duties, he had even begun to forget what she looked like. That is, until this very night when he suddenly recalled that the face one of the veiled mourners in his nightmare bore a striking resemblance to Elspeth's. For some reason unknown to him, he found that to be rather disturbing. He tried to return to sleep but was overcome by a feeling of unease. He decided to get out of bed and read his Bible. His favorite passage was in Exodus and said, "Thou shalt not suffer a witch to live." Those were words by which he lived and earned his daily bread.

The witch-finder made a move to sit up, but he immediately discovered that he was unable to raise his torso more than a few inches before being blocked by some strange obstruction that hovered above in the pitch-blackness of his room. Puzzled by the queerness of this thing, he then attempted to turn himself but found there to be what felt like walls close to his sides. He banged upon them a number of times with his fists in a fruitless effort to break through their restraint.

The walls and roof that surrounded him and afforded him little movement were solid and felt to Matthew to be a rough-hewn wood of some type. They gave off dull thuds in response to his blows but were steadfast in their refusal to budge. The air was now growing uncomfortably warm and steamy.

"What ungodly manner of witchery have I fallen under?" Matthew shouted from within his solid cocoon of darkness. "In the name of the Lord, I command that this cursed spell be at once broken!"

A harrowing minute of silence passed. It felt like an eternity.

Matthew again attempted to sit up, confident in the power of his command, but he found that the mysterious blockade that surrounded his body was still in place, unchanged. He repeated his command, his words fueled by his growing ire. But to his dismay, it was again met by a grim silence that burned within his ears. He then began to wonder if perhaps he was still asleep and this strange predicament was nothing more than part of his foul nightmare. The thought brought some comfort to him, and he lay still and silently prayed to wake up. And then came a faint voice from somewhere above. It was ghostly in its tones yet possessed a strange familiarity about it. It whispered his name, again and again, until Matthew's recognition of it made him shudder. It was the voice of Elspeth.

Matthew's heart began to pound like the fists of a thousand corpses demanding vengeance. It palpitated with such a violent fury that it battered his eardrums and threatened to explode from his chest.

"Witch!" Matthew yelled, flames of anger reddening his face and making prominent the blue veins on his temples. "Do you deny that this sorcery is your doing? Why do you not leave me in peace, foul spirit?"

Elspeth replied with a burst of mocking laughter and then growled, "I shall never leave you in peace, dearly departed husband of mine. I shall remain by your side in hell for all of eternity! That I promise you!" Her voice, once lilt and sweet as a young bird's song, was now a voice possessed of a harsh and venomous tonal quality.

"Dearly departed? But I am not yet dead!" Matthew cried, his lips trembling. "I am very much alive. My heart within my chest continues to beat, albeit in somewhat of a flurry at present." His voice suddenly took on an audacious tone. "I am a servant unto the Lord, and Heaven has reserved a place for my soul."

"Yes, Matthew," Elspeth agreed. "Indeed, you are not yet one of the dead as I am; that much is true. But your time approaches with haste. As for the soul of which you speaketh, you do not possess one. And the only place reserved for you is in hell!" Her laughter once again arose like a tempest, filling Matthew with a sense of dread.

"Hold your tongue, filthy witch!" Matthew cried out, infuriated by the dead woman's insolence. "You are but a fabricator of untruths. Why do you persist in tormenting me in this manner? Are the fires of hell not hot enough to keep you from bewitching my mind with a nightmare of my own burial?"

"Nightmare?" Elspeth chuckled. She found the witch-finder's incomprehension to be a most amusing thing. "No nightmare has plagued your sleep, my husband… my murderer." She went on to explain, "The mourners your eyes saw were quite real. The undertakers who attended to your seemingly lifeless body were quite real. Your burial, as the passage of time will soon convince you, was no figment of the imagination."

Panic had now set in, and Matthew's mind scrambled to form cohesive thoughts. A petrifying numbness was pervading his limbs, deadening his sense of touch, and he was drawing his breaths in short, stabby gasps like a panting dog in hot weather. "But how can that be possible?" he demanded, now realizing that the wood surrounding him actually was a coffin. "How can I continue to breathe as a living man, yet be buried in the cold and dark of the earth as the dead?"

"Don't you know, Matthew?" asked Elspeth in a taunting manner. "When you condemned me as a witch and took pleasure in watching me burn alive, you forgot to take care to remember that I was the only other person who knew the dreadful secret of your cataleptic curse. I'm afraid you've been mistaken for the dead and buried alive, and no one is wise to that fact, save for you and me. It's just our little secret, my love." She roared with vengeful laughter.

Matthew's maddening cry rang out and echoed inside his ears, nearly deafening him. He furiously pounded his fists on the unyielding coffin lid and frantically tried to claw his way out of the wooden funerary box until his fingers were broken and bloodied. Sweat was flowing with profusion from out of his forehead, running down his face, stinging his eyes and bringing a salty taste to his lips. His chest heaved as he desperately gasped for air.

Six feet above, the sound of Elspeth's laughter echoed through the mist-filled graveyard as her ghost tossed a bouquet of wilted flowers on top of her husband's fresh grave, which was marked only by a small wooden cross that stood slightly bent. With a smile on her vaporous face, she turned and slowly walked away as lifeless brown leaves danced in the icy wind. She paused for a moment to take one final look at Matthew's gravesite.

"I'll see you in hell!" she hissed before vanishing into the ethers.

About the Author

N. K. Carlson

N. K. Carlson is an author living in Texas. Originally from the Chicago area, he graduated from the University of Illinois before studying at Logsdon Seminary, where he graduated with a Master of Divinity degree. He has published two books.

The Things that Charm Us and the Smelly Gospel (which was co-written with Drew Doss) both came out in 2020.

His love of writing began in elementary school when each student was given a blank white book to fill with a story. In college, he took an interest in blogging and writing novels.

His debut YA fantasy novel, Shadow and Sword, releases in April 2022.

About the Author

Marie McGrath

Marie McGrath lives in a small rural town in Maryland.

She hopes to inspire others with her stories. Her favorite genres to read are YA Romance and Contemporary Fiction.

She loves the color turquoise, tigers, and listening to music.

About the Author

Alaine Greyson

Alaine Greyson lives outside of Baltimore, Maryland with her husband, son and cocker spaniel puppy.

She loves to push the envelope with her stories and strives to make her readers sympathize with characters from all backgrounds.

Alaine is an avid reader and considers Jane Austen and Diana Gabaldon to be her literary heroes.

She loves Mexican food, 80s music and is a Robert Downey Jr. super-fan.

You will find mentions of things she loves throughout her books.

About the Author

Jinny Alexander

Jinny was first published in Horse and Pony magazine at the age of ten. She's striving to achieve equal accolade now she's(allegedly) a grown up.

Jinny obtained a distinction in an Open University Advance Writing course in 2017, and since then, has had some success with short story and flash competitions. Dear Isobel will be her first published novel. She also has a series of cozy mysteries in the pipeline.

Jinny teaches English as a foreign language to people all over the world. Her home for now is in rural Ireland, which she shares with her husband, a steady stream of visitors from overseas, and far too many animals. Her children are grown and almost independent now. Jinny quite likes to shut the door on all that, and write.

About the Author

Lo Potter

Lo Potter publishes fiction, non-fiction, memoir essays, and poetic works. Previous works include contributions for The Poison Cast podcast; a memoir essay and flash fiction piece in After Alexei; and "Alexithymia in 2020"—Stigma Fighters, May 17, 2020—and many works on CoffeeHouseWriters.com You can find and purchase their recently published collection of poetry "L'identité Politique." Based in the Pacific Northwest, they enjoy spending time with friends and family while searching for moments of laughter hiding in unexpected places.

About the Author

Andrew Parker

Andrew Parker

Andrew Parker has been writing fiction for five years, nonfiction for decades. His writings are comprised of an eclectic mix of novels, short stories, poetry, commentaries, and narratives. A discovery writer, he often finds himself surprised as the first reader of his works, as plot twists and character development unfold. A love of words and a desire to bring positive to readers motivates him to continually pound on the keyboard. Andrew's 'day job' for the past 29 years has been as a mental health and substance use treatment therapist. While he won't ever completely give that up, he hopes to shift more of his time and energy into writing. Other published stories include Shadow Angel, in Personal Bests Journal Issue 1.

About the Author

Gerri R. Gray

Gerri R. Gray is an American novelist, short story writer, editor and a lifelong aficionado of horror, dark humor, and all things bizarre. Her debut novel, The Amnesia Girl (a bizarre tale of two psych ward escapees), was published by HellBound Books in October 2017. Her work has appeared in many journals and anthologies. When she isn't busy writing, she can often be found rummaging through antique shops, exploring haunted houses, or traipsing through old cemeteries with her camera. She lives in upstate New York. For more info, please visit her Amazon author page: https://www.amazon.com/Gerri-R-Gray/e/B076GTZ8XK/

Made in the USA
Middletown, DE
24 September 2021

48102922R00128